The Platinum Collection

Celebrating 20 Years

By Filidh Publishing Authors

Filidh Publishing

The Platinum Collection
Celebrating 20 Years
By Filidh Publishing Authors

Copyright © 2023 Filidh Publishing Corp.
ISBN 978-1-927848- 98-2

Filidh Publishing Corp, Victoria, BC, Canada
Filidhbooks.com

Cover designer: Danny Weeds
(Cover)Photographer: LoveTheWind istockphoto ID:
1009803562
(Interior) Photographer: LittleBee80: istockphoto ID:
1279146926,
(Interior) Photographer: Huseyin Bostanci Istockphoto
ID: 1163901807
(Interior) Photographer: 1971yes Istockphoto ID:
1498105655,
Author photos provided by authors.

Royalty proceeds to StandUpToCancer.ca

*"Some people dream of success, while
other people get up every morning
and make it happen."*
~H. Wayne Huizenga Sr. (former owner of the Miami
Dolphins, Florida Panthers, and the Florida Marlins)

*"A diverse mix of voices leads to better discussions,
decisions, and outcomes for everyone."*
~Sundar Pichai (CEO of Google)

"Why be a star when you can make a constellation?"
~Mariam Kaba (Writer, *'We Do This 'Til We Free Us'*)

Foreword

I wrote and illustrated the cover for my first novel when I was 12 years old. My sixth-grade teacher had the best of the class work "published" and shelved in the elementary school library. Our classmates, other students and teachers could borrow the books to read like *real* books. I remember the excitement of being "published" and fell in love with writing then.

We don't know the impact on those who read our work when we write from the heart and push forward that burning need to communicate our vision and experience. Some write to disturb the status quo; others write to heal their own wounds of life, while some write to inspire change and discussion. Still, others write simply because the words and images in their head demand an outlet.

Since 2003, Filidh Publishing has made finding and mentoring excellent writers a central focus. From the Double Dog Dare Writers' Open Mic events in local coffee shops to the selection of anthology contributions and working with single-author book projects, we have watched that same excitement of being appreciated as a writer on many faces.

In celebration of more than 70 authors and 65 projects, we have curated this wonderful collection of writers with vast yet common experiences from homelands worldwide. The poetry and prose to follow moved and inspired us and demanded to be published.

We begin this collection with poetic voices from the United Kingdom, India, Canada, the United Arab

Emirates, and Zimbabwe. Sharing cultural diversity yet common themes and a sense of oneness within those struggles. The verse is endearing and thought-provoking.

Next, we have some excellent short stories from Canada and the Kingdom of Saudi Arabia with diverse themes pulling visions of several countries far away and in-depth imagery of war, addiction, and trauma on an insightful and compassionate platter. You will be disturbed and filled with empathy. You will find yourself wondering and caring about the people you have encountered in these stories. We hope you will be forever changed by the interaction with the work of these fantastic authors.

At the end of this book, you will find a list of our projects of the past 20 years, and we give that nod and our deepest thanks to all of the authors listed.

Following that, you will find information regarding StandUpToCancer.ca, the charity that will receive all royalty proceeds from purchases of this book. Please donate to them yourself as well if you can do so.

Zoe Duff
Managing Director
Filidh Publishing Corp.
October 2023

Table of Contents

Passionate Poetry

Eclipse of the Soul

by Mademoiselle Noir

Lurking in plain sight,
I watch, I observe,
And then I strike when I deem the time right.
Pulling on your strings,
I make you question your reality.
I make you shout,
I make you scream,
I make you cry till you fall to your knees,
all in hopes that you'd finally accept me.
When you look into the mirror,
I force you to see
That you're not who you thought you'd be.
A sword enclosed
in sheaths of gold,
I shred to pieces
all that you used to know.
In your unknowing, is a knowing,
And in your death, you are again reborn.
Shattered and bruised,
broken and torn,
What was dying becomes a fertile soul.
You flow in rubies and pearls,
You sprout flowers that bloom.
The process is complete;
You are now whole.

Mademoiselle Noir

Fatima Farooq, known in the literary world as Mademoiselle Noir (writing as MissNoir on Reedsy), is a gifted storyteller who derives her creative energy from the allure of nature and the intricate tapestry of human emotions. With a passion for exploring the darker facets of life, Mademoiselle Noir artfully conveys profound sentiments through her poetic prose, leaving readers captivated and deeply moved.

Her literary journey commenced with humble beginnings, composing stories and poems on her phone, which have now flourished into an impressive collection. Her debut story, "Peonies in My Posy," stands as a testament to her storytelling prowess and was published on Reedsy.

Beyond her captivating narratives, Mademoiselle Noir has made her mark in the world of poetry. Six of her finely crafted haikus found their home in the esteemed 'Blossom' anthology, a publication by the renowned 300 South Media Group.

Mademoiselle Noir's writing promises to take readers on a poignant journey through the resplendence of the natural world and the profound intricacies of human emotions. She hopes to forge a profound connection with her readers through her words and create a shared sense of oneness and belonging through her stories and poems, all while taking them on a journey through the alluring paths of the human mind. Madamoiselle Noir lives in the United Arab Emirates.

Forget   by Sara Ashton

Cracks of your profanities viewed by

many - Memories fade, painted blue.

A bad taste lingers, what was bright

Is now dull, no more enchantment

The reality revealed, once I walked

With you, now I ache to forget you.

Sara Ashton

Sara Ashton is a 24 year old English and Creative Writing graduate from the South Wales Valleys, United Kingdom. Sara has been published by the independent press Green Ink Poetry digitally and in print.

Sleeping Beaten   by Melissa Moose

A name wasn't what they called me. What they
called me identified me by the colour of my
skin.
The colour of mud. The colour of faded, lead-
based paint.
The paint on a broken, battered old truck.
I felt drawn to it. Out in a mossy, mushy field
of broken dreams alone.
It sat long enough to sink into the pungent,
thick mud.
Still, it cut a menacing shape in the dim light.
Wind rustling what little grass and sticks
managed to claw skywards.
Plodding toward it through the muck I thought
of hunting in the marshes.
I imagined it heading toward someone on an
empty country lane.
The last set of headlights they'd ever see
coming out of the night.
A night similar to this?
The landscape illuminated by moonlight and
memories.
An unusual chill to the air for this time of year.
As if the warmth of the world had no reason to
come into this field near this junked out,
forgotten wreck.
The smell of soil mixed with the perfume of rot,
oxidizing metal and in my imagination, the
faintest hint of denim.
Peeking inside the window I tasted the dust of
time and motor oil.

Oil that long ago leaked into the ground.
The vintage smells accelerated my imagination.
Till I thought the headlights would blaze to life.
Round yellow eyes in a dark metal face.
Grill twisting into a painful smile.
Lurching forward to drag me into the rusty
earth.
Ridiculous.
The musty air seemed dead.
No living thing could be heard or seen.
The crown jewel of a family of ghosts.
Slowly driving itself into the ground.

Melissa Moose

South American born, Canadian, American raised, artist, photographer, author, domestic violence expert, model, psychologist, outlier and comedian. Melissa writes from the foundation of a loved childhood where technology, education, and nature concurrently converged. Developed in a landscape looking different than everyone else wasn't smooth, but made her sharper. This unique perspective, posture, and programming was built by diametrically opposed elders, and personal refusal to "pop collars". Her pieces gather the traumatic research from the real-life family fallout, bravely bubbly brashly alchemized into therapeutic gold; open source. PTSDD, is her natural response to "life that's one big joke".

Melissa is best resented for interesting hobbies, exotic talents, and un-notably getting fired from a reality show; accused of being "too attractive, interesting, AND single" (Jade Fever, Discovery channel, 2014). She's been the littlest hobo, got'er done, rainbowed, and elicited laughs from jungle to prairies, mountains to ocean-mountains to sky, 33 States, 3 different time periods, 3 British Empires, Hank III, and the fiery religious Moomin stomping grounds of Scandinavia. She does not reside with any of her

"1,000 lonely husbands", but harmoniously lives with music, plants, animals, and most sentient beings that can be relocated without injury. Hunt her down @ Melisscious Moose It's meta to drink the Flavor-Aid.

The Elitist Trail
by Srijani Rupsha Mitra

It originates somewhere you don't even
recognize. Dungeons buried in the past, all self-
proclaiming
Stereotypes in aeons — conditioned so well that
you consider
It fair and right and why not equal.
It is that high school winter that you learn at
your fest — the chasm, the indifference
Of not being the bourgeoisie, at the Peak of the
scale. That sidelining at the party,
Those recurrent arrogant words burbled like silk-
smooth mantras,
Peppered, in pinches of salt, that invoke in you,
the deficiency, of not being
An eloquent English speaker. Those rude
identifications of
Your faulty grammar. It all happens
unconsciously, everything
In the hemisphere that
Evokes less
Awareness, makes us
Believe that this is how things should be, that
obnoxious
Inclination towards believing in the discrimination
as
Something sanctimonious, a love for this
Weird social bottleneck theory, eliminating
All stimuli other than what is the "desirable,"
"affluent." It's just normal how women are
Being pushed in the corners, everytime

There is a call out for equality, There is
Always an imposing structure of the
Imagined falsified meaning, an
Excuse why it is just nothing
Else but just justice.This elitist
Legerdemain that burdens all,
These leading voices that fail to recall
The mesh work of racism in
The workplace, in the crux,
In the roots. In this so-called
Level playing field. And
Sameness repeats, over
And over The elevated
Mounds continue
Hiding the realities,
There appears a
Marie, everytime
From history
Disregarding starving
People, as the
Top–down
Model continue

On Visiting Sanchi   by Srijani Rupsha Mitra

I had a dream of visiting Sanchi

The stupa semicircle, the chhatri enlightening us,
the granite moistened in sunlight and

The shalabhanjikas inviting us into a simplicity
so elegant that it is difficult to escape

We breathe, seek beauty among toranas

And the beautiful baulstraids

In this fantastical world, Buddha sits among
tress and sermons us to pray, to say,

Lighting up the mind is a way to nibbana

We watch the dusk light merging with the stupa
dome

Colours all vibrant cool orange, dusky mango

We pray, midst the hush, encircle the entire
stupa

To know the within, to hear what they call the
inner God, that's you, us and we.

Srijani Rupsha Mitra

I am S. Rupsha Mitra, a poet and writer from Kolkata, India with works published in London Reader, Mekong Review, North Dakota Quarterly, Ekstasis by Christianity Today, Resonate, South Seattle Emerald, Indian Literature, Muse India, Madras Courier, Pif Magazine, Bazinega Zine, Dhaka Tribune, We Have Food At Home Blog. My book of poems titled 'Smoked Frames' is forthcoming from JLRB Press. I love to delve into topics of spirituality in poetry.

The Great Pandemic   by Daphne Matiza

It travelled miles to attack them.
Once divided by race and continents
They fell to the same knees
They cried the same tears, prayed the same
petitions
Created the same distance between themselves
and the ones they loved
Their hugs became venom, their handshakes
poison
Caged by masks on their faces
Graves filled with souls they could not gather to
mourn
Amid the chaos, division disappeared, and they
became one
One people battling one virus with one common
symptom
Uncertainty.

Daphne Matiza

Daphne Matiza is a creative writer and poet who believes in maximizing the use of technology to bring people together and drawing attention to issues that matter. She is passionate about youth empowerment and community development, contributing where she can in society through written word and public speaking. Her journey began at age fourteen, when she won a poetry award in a local newspaper, and she hasn't looked back since. Daphne lives in Harare, Zimbabwe.

Powerful Prose

Bookish
By Monique Jacob

Noah Mason had known for a long time that he wasn't cut out to be a bounty hunter. He didn't like most people, much less tracking them down on purpose and bringing them in to face justice.

He discovered this fact about himself shortly after he'd got his private investigator licence and confronted his first bail jumper, who whipped a rock at Noah's head and gave him a concussion that left his ears ringing for nearly a year.

Noah had always been fascinated by unsolved crimes and cold cases. It was what attracted him to bounty hunting and what kept him looking for criminals who hadn't yet been caught. He would spend weeks online and on the phone tracking down perpetrators, then go into a full-blown anxiety attack when the time came to confront them.

It wasn't until he realized that bounty hunting didn't have to involve running down actual humans that his life began to turn around. He'd been hired by a family to find a copy of a will written by an eccentric grandfather. He'd found the will buried in a box of textbooks but, because the box was one of several in a bidding lot at an auction, he'd had to take home a dozen boxes of books. The surprise came when he got paid not only for returning the will to the grateful family, but also when the local high school bought all the textbooks. He'd also traded two boxes of science fiction novels for a set of used tires for Uncle Jack's truck, and started scouring all the auction houses and junk stores he could find.

Noah sat in the passenger seat of the old pickup and waited while Uncle Jack finished loading boxes into the truck bed. He felt acutely embarrassed while he watched through the side mirror. Uncle Jack was seventy-six, nearly three times Noah's age, and he visibly strained as he lifted each box of heavy books.

Noah scowled at his bandaged hands. The burns were worse than Noah would admit, and he hadn't slept well for the last two nights because of the pain in his blistered palms. He knew that Jack would argue if he tried to help with loading as he'd burned his hands putting out a fire that had gotten out of Jack's control. Luckily, his fingertips were spared and he could manage most tasks, including when he sent a text to his librarian friend, Miss Elsie, about the book he'd found in one of the boxes he'd casually looked through while waiting for Jack to arrive with the truck.

The book sat on his lap, water-stained and missing its back cover. On a normal day, a damaged book would be tossed into the burn box to make fire logs, but this book's title, *Deadly Gardens: A Compendium of Poisonous Plants*, had grabbed his attention. Even better, it was a library book, and Noah had returned dozens of overdue library books that he'd found among the thousands of books he'd bought at auctions.

Noah had carefully separated the water-damaged library checkout card from its paper pocket so he could check the date it was due, and discovered a folded letter stuck to the back. It would take steam and patience to unfold the letter, so he'd left it between the book's pages and sent the book's code and due date to the librarian. The book had been checked out 28 years ago, and was the oldest overdue library book he'd ever found!

The driver's door opened with a metallic creak and Uncle Jack dropped into his seat. He groaned and rolled his shoulders before cranking the old engine to life. He pulled away from the loading dock and turned right onto Hammond Road before smiling at Noah and nodding toward the book on his lap.

"Now, let's get that book to the library." Jack smoothed a hand over his thin hair and accelerated, leaning over the steering wheel as if to make the truck go faster.

"We can't go to the library with you looking like that," Noah said with a laugh. "You've got sweaty patches under your arms, and you smell like you've just loaded a truck. It's not like you made such a great impression on her the first time you met, so a bath and shave would be a start. Besides, I've already texted her the details about the book, so we don't have to go right away. She'll probably just tell me to recycle it because it's so old and damaged."

"Old and damaged, eh?" Jack studied his face in the rear-view mirror. He scratched at his unshaven chin, thinking that Noah might be right - at least about the shave. "Then there better be more library books in those boxes. And don't waste too much time looking; there's only water for one good wash this week and I'd like to smell nice long enough to make a fresh impression on Miss Elsie."

"Don't worry; even if we don't have any new overdue books for her, she'll definitely want to see this letter."

"How do you know it's a letter and not just some invoice?"

Noah pinched the folded paper between his unbandaged fingertips and held it up so the light shone through the stained creases.

"I can make out the word 'Beloved,' so it's got to be a love letter."

Uncle Jack beamed at Noah and stomped the gas pedal, making the truck rattle as it bounced over the cracked pavement. He slalomed around the deep pit in the middle of what used to be the main intersection of the business district. The crater, now filled with rubble and garbage, was one of dozens created in the last hours of the Nine-Day War, when rival gangs had fired stolen shells at each other until they ran out of bombs that actually worked. It had pretty much signaled the end of the conflict, though a few pockets of well-armed diehards held out until the military sent in target drones to drop a paralytic gas on each group of holdouts.

The weeks following the Nine-Day War were marked by silence, and the rest of the country gaped at the televised horror, at the long line of cars inching out of Vancouver's core. Thousands of citizens had died, nearly every government building had suffered major damage, and many of the roads were impassable.

"So, do you think there might be much else of value in those boxes?" Jack asked, as he pulled up to the wooden platform where Noah had built a system of hand-pulleys to lift boxes up to the fourth floor of their building.

"I hope so," Noah said. "I saw a few fantasy novels in there so I might be able to complete that series Howard is collecting, and one of the boxes had some school books – science and math, I think. Someone will want those, depending on the level. Miss Elsie will know." He knew that would make Uncle Jack smile, and was not disappointed. Noah hopped out of the truck but wasn't able to manage the pulley gearbox with his bandaged hands and paced while Jack unloaded the truck and set the mechanism to raise the deck.

Jack was not Noah's uncle but neither of them had any living relatives and each had become the other's family after Jack found Noah sleeping in a closet on the top floor of the building that he used to manage. The pricey lawyers and realtors that once filled the building had fled when the conflict broke out, and none returned when the smoke cleared. There were fewer than 20,000 people now living in Vancouver, and Noah hoped folks would move back to the city when grocery store shelves filled up again.

The platform slowly inched up to the fourth floor, where Eddie waited with Jack's dog, Riley.

"Uncle Jack! Did you find any comic books?"

Jack leaned close to Noah. "I might have promised him first pick of any comics we found if he watched Riley for the afternoon."

"We haven't checked all the boxes yet," Noah said to the boy, "but if you help me carry some of them to my room, you can have the special comic I was saving up for later."

"I'll carry all of them!" Eddie jumped down to the platform before it stopped moving and stumbled into Noah, who tried not to gasp in pain when he reached out a hand to stop the boy from pitching over the edge.

The boxes were too heavy for the eight-year-old boy, so Jack opened one and handed four large books to Eddie, who staggered under their weight to Noah's suite with the dog barking and running ahead.

"I'll get the cart for the rest of these or it'll take forever to unload," Jack said. "Then I want a look at that hand again."

"Don't worry about me. It just stings a bit, and I'm annoyed that I'm making you deal with all these boxes. I don't want you to drop dead of a stroke or something."

"Who are you, my mother?" Jack grumbled. "How about you stop watching me sweat and go help the boy clear some space for these boxes. I'm still good for a couple decades yet."

Noah grinned and hopped off the platform. "Fine, it looks like you've got it under control."

"Exactly. I'll get these loaded up on the cart and bring them over in a few minutes. Your only job will be to go through the boxes and find more overdue library books so we have a good reason to visit with Miss Elsie. You found one; there's bound to be more."

Noah followed Eddie to the series of interconnected offices that Jack had assigned to him when they first met. They had spent weeks delivering desks, chairs, and glass-fronted cabinets to the auction house for resale, and had made enough money to have an electrician restore power to their living areas and install the solar panels that they'd scrounged from another abandoned building.

"Hey, Eddie, slow down," he said, as the boy ran past him to get more books. "Uncle

Jack can bring the boxes with the cart. Right now, I need your help to make room for the new books."

"Do you really think there's more comics? I already read all the ones you gave me last time."

"I don't know yet, but you can help me check." Noah hoped there were more than just comics. He'd been teaching Eddie to read, and the boy was ready for something a bit more challenging. Comics engaged him but didn't have much substance. The boy would need stronger reading skills if he were to join the mixed-grade classroom of kids when the regional teacher arrived next month. They'd only have two days to test Eddie and assign him enough homework to help him catch up until the teacher's next visit.

Noah put *Deadly Gardens* on the table and unplugged the lamp from his only working electrical outlet so that he could boil a kettle of water. Every task took longer than usual because of his bandaged hands, but he was getting used to it, and he had Eddie to help with anything that didn't involve fire or electricity.

"Take those newspapers off that bottom shelf and stack them in a pile right next to the log-making tools under the window," Noah said to Eddie, who rushed to do as he was asked. Noah knew the pile would be crooked and likely to slide and spread all over the floor, but he could straighten it up later when the boy had gone to bed.

Eddie was always eager to help and would race to do a task often without waiting for the rest of the instructions. When Noah had burned his hands, Uncle Jack had tasked Eddie with helping Noah as his valet. This led to confusion for Eddie, as he'd heard "ballet" and proceeded to whirl and dance around Noah, much to Jack's amusement.

Jack had found Eddie several months ago while out scavenging in an abandoned store with Riley. The dog had become very interested in a pile of crumpled cardboard boxes. Eddie had screamed in terror when Jack pulled him out of the nest of rotting food containers and mouldy blankets, starved and covered in lice and fleas.

A few days after they'd cleaned him up and given him all the food he could eat, the boy took them to the docks, where they found the corpses of six adults in a half-burned boat. There wasn't much left to identify them, but Eddie pointed out his parents and two uncles. He didn't know who the others were or what had happened to the other four children who fled with him when the bad men came on board. The children ran in different directions to cause confusion, as they'd been taught, but Eddie had been unable to find any of them after the men had gone. He also had no idea how long he'd been hiding, but Jack estimated the bodies had been decomposing for weeks.

Eddie came over to watch what Noah was doing after he finished stacking newspapers.

"Do you need more shelves cleared out? We're gonna need lots and lots of space for all these boxes!" He bounced on his toes as he watched Noah holding some paper over the steam that rose from the hot kettle. He reached for the book with the colourful cover but pulled his hand back when Noah shook his head.

"First, let's see what we've got, and then we can decide how much space we need," Noah said, as he carefully unfolded the sheet of stained paper. It was definitely a handwritten letter, written in ink, that hadn't run when the paper got wet.

Eddie ran to the door when they heard the rumble of the cart and Uncle Jack whistling his usual melancholy tune. It was a series of seven ascending notes, whistled over and over. He said it was all he remembered of his late wife's favourite song. He was afraid of forgetting it, so he diligently whistled it. Noah was pretty sure that it was several notes longer when he first met Jack but had never pointed out to his friend that his song was getting shorter.

Noah peeled the last fold apart and set the letter on the table, flattening it with a heavy book. It was fragile, and the paper had crumbled in the folds, obscuring some of the writing. He was faintly embarrassed to be reading a personal letter, especially when it was addressed to "My Beloved". Probably just a love letter, but why was it hidden in a book about poisons?

He gave Eddie his knife so he could cut the tape that held each box shut, and turned away pointedly to show that he trusted the boy with the knife. Noah knew that Eddie would be careful but worried that he would accidentally score the cover of a valuable book. It was a chance he was willing to take, and felt that it was a better lesson to let Eddie damage a book and explain later rather than micromanage the boy's enthusiasm.

"What are you looking for this time?" Eddie bent back the top flaps of a box and peered inside. "A boring diary again? More school books?"

"Nothing specific. Just stack everything on the shelves or on the floor if you run out of space, and I can sort through it all later." Noah hoped to find at least one title listed in his notebook. It had been a month since he'd found that boxed set of encyclopedias and brought it to the reconstructed high school at the edge of the city. The books were outdated, but the teachers were so grateful to have them that they gave Noah three bags of vegetables from the student gardens. Noah, Eddie, and Uncle Jack had happily eaten mashed potatoes and boiled corn every day for a week.

Noah's notebook contained many lists. The high school had asked for science and math textbooks, and the tiny college attached to Miss Elsie's library had begged him to find any kind of instruction manuals relating to electricity or plumbing. He also kept several lists of fictional series that various friends and clients had asked him to complete.

Eddie opened another box and gasped. "Noah, you gotta see this!" He grunted as he struggled to lift out a large book. He staggered over to Noah and thumped it onto the table.

Noah sighed and shook his head. A bible. A huge, hardcover King James bible.

"These big ones are worth a lot, right?"

"Yeah, but I really hate them." Noah grimaced and flipped open the cover, gingerly turning the thin pages with his fingertips. The bible was in excellent condition and was a valuable find.

But church people were the worst. Before they paid him for the bible, they would expect him to stay for dinner, which would be delicious but would involve many prayers and at least one sermon. They would thank him profusely for bringing them such a valuable gift and would call him Brother, as if he were one of them.

Maybe Jack would agree to get saved this time.

Noah closed the bible and turned back to the letter, which was easier to handle after being steamed and flattened. It was plain paper, the kind you put in old copiers, stained but mostly legible. His eyes widened as he read.

"What's it say?"

Noah was grateful that Eddie couldn't read the cursive handwriting. "It's just a mushy love letter," he said, and was relieved when Eddie rolled his eyes and went back to emptying boxes.

It was only a half-truth because the letter, which did begin with a declaration of love, was obviously a suicide note. It was filled with profuse apologies to a wife and son, and contained means, motive, and coordinates in northern Ontario where a terminally ill man named Philip had killed himself nearly three decades ago.

"...I couldn't bear to put you through the trauma of watching me die slowly while our savings disappeared. If I could go back and change things, get a big insurance policy maybe, I would have done anything to spare you from the medical bills this cancer was going to bring.

"...brewed a gentle cocktail of pain drugs that Dr. Sampson gave me, along with a few petals and leaves stolen from the poison plants garden at the University.

"...a system of caves 12 kms north of Smokey Falls. I haven't been there since I was a teenager but am quite certain I can find them again..."

Noah set down the letter and watched Eddie stack paperbacks against the wall next to the full shelf. He could see several science fiction titles that he was sure were on one of his lists. Those books, along with the bible, made this one of his better auction days. He'd be able to afford more wood for the big stove, and not be so reliant on the newspaper logs that took so much time to make.

He checked the due date on the library book again just as his cell phone rang. He struggled to hold the phone without dropping it as he accepted the call.

"Hello, Noah," the excited voice said breathlessly. "It's Elsie. From the library. You're not going to believe this! Your book is from a library in Princeton. Ontario! That's near Brampton in the southern half of the province. But the best part, which is actually quite tragic, is that the borrower, Philip Winter, disappeared a week before the book was due."

"He killed himself." Noah spoke quietly so Eddie wouldn't hear.

"What? Are you sure? How do you know?"

"There's a suicide note in the book. It's signed Philip and is clearly a letter to his wife."

"That's marvellous!" Elsie exclaimed. "I mean not really, but hold on there's more here." Noah heard rustling paper and Elsie muttering excitedly.

"When he disappeared, there was talk of murder, and his wife was interrogated and then released. She was so appalled that anyone would think she had killed her husband, that as soon as the police cleared her, she packed up the house and took her son west. You'll never guess where!" Elsie didn't stop long enough for an answer and kept talking, explaining that she'd done a couple of internet searches and found several old articles about the missing man and how after his wife had moved away the case went cold and everyone seemed to forget about it.

Noah reached over to where Eddie had stacked magazines that he'd found in one of the boxes, and picked up an issue of the *Princeton University Student Magazine*. It was in mint condition, and had likely sat in the box for 28 years without being disturbed.

"Was Philip connected with Princeton University?"

"Yes, the articles say that he was the university's groundskeeper for many years before he disappeared. He was also taking part-time courses. Didn't you hear what I just said? His wife and son moved here! Right here!"

"It looks like the boxes I bought today are full of his stuff. There are magazines from Princeton, and a couple more overdue library books from the same year.

"This is so exciting! I can hardly stand it," Elsie said. She took a deep breath. "There's even an obituary, and it looks like the son still lives here. There are several David Winters listed locally, so I wrote down the numbers for you. It's too much excitement for this old gal, so I'll leave it to you to decide if you should call him or the police with this information." She slowly read out three phone numbers, and Noah entered them into his phone before saying goodbye.

He put the phone down just as Uncle Jack walked into the room with his freshly clean hair plastered against his scalp.

"Uncle Jack," Eddie called. "I found six comics! They're Batmans! All of them!"

"That's great, kiddo. Let me know if you find any words you need help with." Jack chuckled as Eddie raced past him, heading for the "secret" room where he kept his prized possessions, mostly comic books and random broken toys.

Noah waited until the boy had left the room.

"Close the door so he doesn't hear this, okay?" Noah hooked a second chair with his foot and slid it to the table where the book on poisons sat next to the suicide note. He sat and waited for Jack to join him.

"So, did you find any more library books?" Jack asked expectantly. "Do we get to visit Miss Elsie later?"

"Yeah, there are at least two more besides this one," Noah said. He smiled at Jack's expression. Jack had been sweet on Elsie for years but had never worked up the nerve to tell her. "We can go deliver them tomorrow, but right now, I need you to help me decide what to do about this letter." He slid the suicide note to where Jack was sitting and watched his friend's eyes widen as he read.

"Holy cats! Are we the first ones to see this?"

"Looks like it. This note's been hidden for almost thirty years. No one ever laid eyes on it after he wrote it or they would have found his body." Noah told him about the family's move from Ontario to the west coast after Philip Winter's disappearance.

"He probably expected someone to return the library book and notice the suicide note. But how did it get into a bunch of random boxes at the auction house?"

"His wife packed up all his stuff and took it with her when she moved here," Noah explained.

"What do you mean here?"

Noah showed him the list of phone numbers and the news articles that Elsie had sent him by text. "The family moved here and probably put away the boxes with Philip's stuff and never opened them again. Then his wife died recently, and the son emptied the house and sent most of it to auction."

"But that means..."

"It means I have a clue that solves a missing person cold case."

The two men stared at each other for a moment, then down at the letter again.

"This is like real police work," Uncle Jack said. "You better get this solved soon so we have more news to impress Miss Elsie. Hey, maybe there will be a reward," he continued as he got up and slapped Noah on the back.

Noah was filled with excitement. Jack was right; this felt like real police work. Noah had studied for a private investigator license so he could at least be a part of helping his community in some small way. It was a less exciting way to make a living than being one of the uniformed men who now patrolled the area on horses, but he'd managed to locate many missing documents and valued possessions that brought peace to families forced to flee when the gang war broke out.

He'd spent years scouring auctions and junk stores, persevering even when a tip led to nothing but boxes of mouldy newspapers and magazines.

But this time Noah's dogged patience had paid off and he'd found an actual missing person. The coordinates in the letter would lead the Ontario police to the body. He carefully re-folded the letter and tucked it into the book to keep it safe. The police would want it as evidence, but he decided to contact the family first. They would want to know that their loved one had finally been found.

Noah didn't care about any reward. The excitement he felt at the small part he'd played in solving this mystery was the best bounty of all.

Noah picked up the phone and called the first number on the list.

Monique Jacob

Monique Jacob is a member of the Eclectic WritersBootcamp and makes regular appearances at the Double Dog Dare Writers' Open Mic events.. Born in Germany, Monique has moved 29 times in 9 cities and now makes her home on Vancouver Island.

Bookish was inspired by a June 2022 story on the CBC National News, about a library book that was borrowed from the Tooting Library in UK in 1974, ended up in a box in Belcarra, BC and was mailed back to the UK nearly five decades overdue.

Monique Jacob is the author of *Tye Dye Voodoo, Voodoo Mystery Tour*, and the upcoming *Voodoo Café*. She has also published *Bright Light*, a sci-fi alien abduction novel for teens, and has contributed several short stories to other charitable anthologies published by Filidh Publishing. Monique was, in fact, motivational in the development of the first anthology, .and the charity connection.

She can be found reading from her recent works at local cafés and public libraries. You can also follow Monique Jacob on Facebook at *https://www.facebook.com/AuthorMoniqueJacob/*.
(Photo credit: Geoectomy)

Dead Boat
by Terry Groves

"Rhonda Smith?" the police officer asked from the doorstep.

"Y-yes," Rhonda stammered through the half-open door.

"I need you to come with me."

"Why?"

"I have a warrant here." He held up a folded paper.

Rhonda's chest burned as her vision narrowed. It was hard to draw breath. She wished her parents were home. Even her older brother Ron would have been of some help. *Is this going to make me miss school tomorrow?*

After a moment of pondering questions she might ask, things she might say, she stepped outside. She knew why the police were there. As she lost herself in the memories that led to this moment, the voice of the officer faded. "I have to handcuff you..."

* * *

Rhonda stretched her neck, trying to see inside the windows of the derelict boat as they cruised by. *Was that curtain moving, disturbed by a skeletal hand or dry, harsh corpse breath?* She leaned over the side railing of their own boat, peering into the reflections on the glass.

"Rhonda," her father barked. Surprise shot through her heart, raising her pulse to pounding status. She fumbled for a handhold as she over-balanced, almost dropping her camera. Her head snapped toward her dad. "The bumpers should be out by now." He stood at the helm, guiding their boat into the marina, toward their slip.

Rhonda raised her camera and took several quick shots of the decrepit boat as it fell behind them. Then she turned her attention to her first-mate duties. Fourteen was two years away from being trusted enough to be allowed to captain the boat, and she had a lot to learn before she could do what her dad did. Sometimes, when it was calm and there weren't a lot of boats around, he would let her command their 36-foot Sea Ray. Once, she even got to launch it while he handled the lines to cast off. Mostly though, she did what he told her, and did it fast. She loved to be on the water and was happy to earn the day cruises. But that old boat bothered her.

"Dad," Rhonda spoke from the dock as she checked the mooring lines. "How long has that old boat been at that buoy?"

"Which one?" Her dad scanned the harbour, one hand shielding his eyes from the late afternoon sun.

"The dea--", Rhonda caught herself. She'd almost called it the dead boat, the name christened by her brother Ron two weeks ago. She recalled that day.

* * *

"Look," Ron called from the stern of their inflatable tender. He'd had his boat license for two years, and Dad let him take this one out whenever he wanted. They were returning with their catch of prawns. He pointed. "It's the dead boat," letting his voice drop in an ominous tone.

Rhonda twisted in her seat at the front. She'd been watching him steer, using the handle on the motor. Being jealous that she wasn't the one in control felt immature, but he never followed the rules, and he drove too fast. She wouldn't ignore the rules, but just because she was younger, she wasn't considered trustworthy. She'd been thinking about that when he spoke. "I think there's a dead body on there."

Uncertain she had heard him right, Rhonda asked, "What do you mean?"

"That's why it's in such crappy shape." Ron pointed his chin toward the beige hull, drifting on its tether, mauve canvas, streaked with green and black goop. "No one to clean off the bird crap and moss."

"It is in rough shape." She studied the faded wood trim and scarred fiberglass, but it was the stained canvas that looked the worst. Slimy moss spilled down the sides.

"No one's polished the rails or the deck for ages. It's a rotting corpse. It's a dead boat."

And that nickname was embedded in Rhonda's mind.

* * *

"The derelict-looking one, there, with the purple helm." She pointed, but Dad was already looking in that direction.

"I don't know," he said, as though seeing the boat for the first time. "It's been there quite a while. I guess at least two years. Why?"

"I was just wondering why someone would let their boat get like that."

Her dad looked across the water for a few moments, then along the line of boats in their moorage. Rhonda followed his gaze, taking in the many types, power and sail, wood and fiberglass, big and small, in all states of care.

"Some people don't know much about boating when they get into it. It is more work than they like to do or can afford. Maybe whoever owns that boat doesn't like life on the water and can't sell it."

"Yeah." Rhonda looked at her dad's face, noticing the deep lines carved by long hours in the sun and wind.

"Maybe the owner died or got sick, and no one else wanted to take it over."

"Ron says there's a body on the boat."

"Ron reads too much Stephen King."

"You don't think someone could have died on that boat, and no one knows?"

"Possible, but I doubt it. There'd be a

smell."

"Yeah." Rhonda stared at the dead boat even after her father headed toward the ramp leading to the shore.

At home, after downloading the photos from her camera to her computer, she studied the ones of the dead boat. The moss, the age, the neglect was apparent. Then she noticed something in one window. Zooming into that part, she leaned in close to the screen, her nose almost touching it. A face appeared. A shock blasted in her chest, across her shoulders. Her heart thumped. She jerked back, crying, "Oh."

Her head slammed into something as two hands gripped her shoulders. She screamed and jerked forward.

"What'cha looking at, Sis?"

"You bugger," Rhonda's heart pounded against her ribcage. She could picture it gulping great gouts of blood. It had just been Ron's face reflected in her screen. "I almost peed my pants."

"Did I scare you?" Ron smirked.

"You know you did." Rhonda tapped the

flat of her hand on her chest, trying to settle her heart.

"Got ya good." Ron turned to the computer screen. "But seriously, what are you looking at?"

"It's the dead boat."

"Really?"

"Yeah, it's...," then she realized he was being sarcastic. "You are a bugger." She slapped his arm. "I took this photo today. Look at the window. Do you see it?"

"See what?" Ron leaned in close.

"There." She pointed.

"Let's see." Ron leaned over her shoulder.

"Nice photo, Sis. Even blown up like this, it's in focus." Ron hummed while he looked, tapping a finger against his throat. In the image on the screen, white lacey curtains arced across the window, but at the very edge was a shape.

"Are those feet?" Rhonda asked.

"Propped up, like the ankles are crossed?" Ron offered.

"Red striped socks," Rhonda added.

"Like someone relaxing." Ron stood upright.

"Could someone have died reclining, and no one realized?" She turned to look at her brother. *That would be terrible. All alone like that. Spooky too.*

"Hope so," Ron displayed a cruel grin. "That'd be so cool."

He's not that mean, is he? He must be kidding. Right?

That night, as Rhonda set sail on the slumber sloop, those socks drifted in her mind.

***

The next day, following an early morning rain, Rhonda paddled her kayak toward the dead boat. Damp coolness clung to the day, raised goosebumps down her arms. There was a tightness in her chest, but she had to know about that boat; had to discover its secrets. Skimming toward it, something didn't seem right, but Rhonda couldn't figure out what it was.

Before she could settle what was wrong, she was close to the swim grid at the stern.

She saw the faded words, Better Life, in a small arc across the transom. *Better Life? Well, that's an appropriate name. It has certainly seen better days.* Turning the kayak at the last moment, she brought it alongside and reached for a handhold. After tying the two boats together, she climbed from one to the other. Standing, she looked at the dead boat. *Does it really contain a corpse?* But that was probably just Ron's over-active imagination. *What if he's right?*

Rhonda sighed and slumped her shoulders. *I'll deal with it. I'll just deal with it.* Gripping the salt-caked ladder handle, she climbed to the afterdeck.

The sun hadn't risen high enough to flood this area, but the faded fabric of two deck chairs awaited another day's sun bleaching. Their scarred wooden arms looked brittle and were the colour of bone. The rotting carpet, worn through in spots, was testament to the harsh sea air and bitter winter winds. Green slime coated much of the exposed deck, lay slick under her feet. Rhonda kept her hands close, not wanting to touch anything.

"This may not be one of my brighter ideas," she whispered, afraid of what she might disturb if she spoke too loud. Even as she breathed the words, she knew she couldn't stop. Something drew her into the boat, urging her. She stepped across the deck, reaching for the rough, corroded cabin door handle. *Hatch,* she corrected herself. O*n a boat, it's a hatch.* She twisted the latch, but it didn't turn.

"Of course, it's locked," she muttered, looking around the deck space. "Like, everyone would want to steal *this* boat."

She chuffed at her wit, wondering if she could force the door, *hatch*, open. Might as well turn her trespass into a full-fledged break and enter. *Juvie Hall for a decrepit old boat. I must be nuts.* Then she saw the deck box. *What might be in there? Certainly not cleaning supplies. Maybe a key?*

No way it could be that easy. She stepped to the locker and fumbled with the latch. Locked too. No, just stuck. It popped open. Raising the lid, she peaked inside. A snake. She recoiled. No, just a coil of electric wire, the scales just overlapping spider webs woven into a veritable blanket. Thick spider egg nests made up the serpent's eyes. Loops of rope, a fishnet, and bottles of who knew what surrounded the faux serpent. And there, barely visible in the corner was a yellow float key fob. Rhonda brushed aside the webs, cautious of any movement that might be a spider. They may be small, but their hairy legs and tiny mandibles freaked her out. She grabbed the fob and rushed back to the hatch.

It took a bit of work, but the key ground its way into the lock. Rhonda pushed on the door, turning the key with a gentle hand, jiggling it back and forth, then applying more pressure to free the mechanism. Afraid of snapping the key off, but also feeling urgency, not wanting to be seen entering this boat that was not hers, Rhonda twisted harder. The key was going to break, twist off. Then the latch moved, rasping, sending sandpaper vibrations into her fingers. With a snick, the door loosened, then swung toward her. The hatchway loomed. The dim interior beckoned.

Stale, dusty air wafted from inside. As

Rhonda stared into the waiting cabin, the boat's salon, she thought she knew how archaeologists felt when opening a newly discovered Egyptian tomb. While the outside of the boat showed the ravage of the damp West Coast climate, the interior puffed of desert breezes. *Perfect atmosphere to preserve the dried-out husk of a long-dead corpse.* "Shut up, Ron," she whispered, even though he was just a voice in her head. The stairs creaked as she stepped down *into the crypt.*

The air swallowed the light as though it was moisture on sunbaked wood. The cries of the gulls and murmur of water faded; afraid to invade this mausoleum. Rhonda stepped full into the cabin and turned to where her photo had captured the crossed feet.

There was no corpse reclining with its feet up, not even a chair to sit in. The space was the galley, and what she had thought were feet, was a pair of oven mitts hung on a hook. As her eyes adjusted to the dim light, filtered by the filthy windows, the shapes of the furniture and decorations became more defined. Rhonda explored the cabin.

* * *

"My parents?" Rhonda looked up at the officer, who held her by the upper arm.

"They're being notified." He guided her to the squad car, idling at the curb, the rear door open. He placed a hand on her head as she bent to enter. "Watch your noggin." The door closed, locking her inside.

Rhonda laid her head against the window. The car rocked, and the driver's door slammed. Then they pulled into traffic. Could what she had done be so bad that it came to this? Trespassing on a derelict boat hardly seemed worth this attention. She didn't look out the window as the patrol car wove its way through the streets, afraid someone who knew her would see her here in her guilt. She hardly noted when the vehicle came to a stop, and the engine died.

* * *

Thick dust and cobwebs coated everything, but there was a tidiness to the arrangement that gave a feminine feeling. There was no clutter; even the books on a shelf were organized by size. Rhonda felt a woman's influence in the boat. She moved about, avoiding touching anything, to keep the dust down but mostly to avoid disturbing any creepy crawlies. As she grew familiar with the space, her curiosity about the owner grew, too. *Who would be so meticulous about this portable home and then just abandon it?*

A thick book lay on a side table. It's homemade fabric cover, edged with once white, now gray, lace. She brushed at the dust on it. *Our Boating Life* was stitched into the cover. She flipped it open.

The pages were clean, protected by the cover. Black and white photos of the boat, in much better shape, and a young family smiled at her. Parents and three kids, two young girls and a boy, standing in bathing suits, posing. The caption, *New Summer Home,* was printed in meticulous handwriting beneath the photo. Rhonda studied the faces. The parents' expressions reflected pride and eagerness. The kids looked bored, perhaps eager to be somewhere else.

Rhonda turned the page. More photos, more tidy printing detailing places, first names, activities. Rhonda turned another page, another, another. The photos changed to colour ones. She became lost in the old records of the boat's family. Through the many photos, maps, diagrams, and brief captions, the family of the boat came to life. It chronicled their adventures and how their love of the water grew over the years. The children grew into teens, then young adults, then faded from the records, presumably to grow their own families. The last few pages showed only the parents, mostly only one in each photo, as the other must have been behind the camera. They had grown old, with the same deep lines in their faces that Rhonda saw in her own father. The last photo showed the couple, the mother now in a wheelchair on a dock. Then a hand grabbed her shoulder.

Rhonda's chest jumped. She screamed, dropping the book. She twisted, pulling away, raising a fist.

"Hey, Sis." Ron grinned at her with another cruel smile. He knew he had scared her, had intended to.

"You bastard." She wanted to punch

him, but that would only feed his enjoyment. Instead, she picked up the book, checking to see if it was damaged, while her heartbeat settled.

"Thought you would be here." Ron flashed a sincere smile at her. "So, where's the body?"

Resisting an urge to strangle him, she settled for delivering disappointment. "There isn't one. Just the story of a family who loved boating. It's all here in this album."

Ron looked around the cabin, touched a few of the decorations with his fingertips. Then he sniffed and turned back to his sister.

"Family of spiders looks like."

"I recognize some of the places in the photos, Charles Cove, Big Beach Island, even some of our secret spots up in Desolation Sound." Rhonda looked at Ron, brushing at the album cover with her pinky finger. "But I don't recognize one spot. It's in a lot of the photos, a marina. I think it's where they moored the boat."

"Let me see." Ron reached for the album.

Rhonda twisted, keeping it away. Instead, she turned to a page that showed what appeared to be the beginning of a trip. Most of the family was on the dock, one kid on the front of the boat. They were putting supplies on for a voyage. There were many boats in the background, noses pointing into the dock.

"Hmmm," Ron studied the photos, "I don't recognize it either, or any of the boats. But I think I can read a couple of their names."

Ron looked at Rhonda as though studying her face. Then he smiled one of his genuine smiles, the ones that made Rhonda happy he was her brother. "Google girl," he called her by the name he used when he wanted to remind her about her computer skills. "Maybe you can use that to figure out what marina they moored at."

"Yea," Rhonda's eyes widened. Why hadn't she thought of that? From there, it should be easy to figure out who the family is. Maybe she could locate them, find out why they abandoned the boat. "I need to go home and use my computer."

Searching Google, using the photos of the marina, she figured out it was a small one, a hundred kilometers north. Phoning there, offering the boat's name, they gave her a last name. Running that through Facebook with some of the first names from the album led her to one of the girls, now a grown adult. Admitting her trespass on their boat and explaining what she had found, she got an address to mail the album to. That was all the woman was interested in. Hadn't even asked about the boat and, in her excitement at finding the family, Rhonda forgot to ask the one question she wanted answered. *Why did they abandon the boat?* Being embarrassed about her transgression, she was reluctant to contact them again. Maybe getting the album would confirm her motives, encourage forgiveness for her unlawful intrusion.

And now this, Rhonda raised her head from the cool glass of the police cruiser window. *Guess I was wrong.*

Looking around, she thought, *This isn't the police station.* "Where are we?"

"Scene of the crime." The officer glanced at her, then opened his door and climbed out. Then, her mind grasped her surroundings. *The Marina.*

A few moments later, her door opened. The officer guided her out of the car. When he stepped to one side, Rhonda saw a group of people near the car, on the side opposite the docks. She saw her parents and stepped toward them. Tears stung her eyes. She said, "I'm sorry...," but her words stopped when the officer tugged her arm. Her parents were smiling. *Smiling?* She looked around at the other people. Everyone was smiling. *What is going on?*

The officer led her through the crowd, onto the grassy area across the road from the marina. There was a podium, and beside that, the police chief and two other officers, all dressed in their best uniforms, sharp, crisp and shiny. *Am I on the most wanted list?* Turned to face the crowd; there was a click and tug, then her hands were free of the cuffs. Rubbing her wrists, she saw everyone staring at her. Heat rose in her neck, flushed her cheeks.

The police chief spoke in a loud, stern voice. "It is important that our young people learn the consequences of their actions." *He's going to make an example of me. But why is everyone smiling?*

"This young lady went onto property that didn't belong to her, a boat. Then she took something, something that also didn't belong to her." The chief paused for a moment and looked at Rhonda. "And then she went to great lengths to find out who these things belonged to." Again, he paused and looked over his shoulder, nodding to someone behind him. "The rest of this lesson comes from someone else."

Rhonda turned to where the Chief had looked. She saw a tall man striding toward her. Something familiar about him, like she had known him a long time ago.

He stopped beside her, placed his hands on each side of the podium, and spoke. "I am Scott Mulgrew. I grew up in a boating family. We spent our summers on the water, like many of you." He looked over the crowd. "It was a wonderful childhood, a great way to

72

grow up." There were murmurs from the crowd.

Scott paused, and Rhonda looked up at him. She studied the lines of his face, saw a tear on his cheek. As he continued to speak, she recognized him. *He was in the photos. Only much younger.* Her face burning, Rhonda knew it was serious if he had traveled all this way.

"My mother, Mary Mulgrew, documented our boating adventures in an album. It contained all those summers, all those memories. Eventually, we kids left home, but she and Dad continued to love their boat, *Better Life*. Even after Mom lost the ability to walk, they boated." Scott sucked in a large breath.

"Dad passed suddenly." His voice cracked. He brushed his cheek with the back of a hand, let out a long sigh, then continued in a steadier tone. "Mom developed Alzheimer's. As her memory faded, so did our history. The boat got lost. We think Mom had it moored and then forgot that memory. The most devastating part of this was losing the album."

Scott turned and looked at Rhonda. He squeezed his eyes shut, and more tears streamed down his face. *He doesn't look angry.* Blinking twice, he continued speaking.

"Rhonda sent us the album. She returned my ... our childhood. It felt like a miracle, but the real miracle was still to come. When we showed the album to Mom," Rhonda heard a noise behind her and turned to see the woman from the last photo being wheeled beside her, "she came back. Whenever she holds the album," it lay in the woman's lap, the cover now bright and clean, "my mother," the man's voice wavered, then returned, "comes back."

Scott turned to Rhonda, placed a hand on her shoulder, and spoke, looking into her eyes. Rhonda knew the tears in her eyes were for the words he had spoken, not the admonishment he was about to deliver.

"You gave us back our childhood. You gave us back our mother." With that, he hugged Rhonda. She didn't resist. She didn't resist when he turned her toward his mother. The old woman held out her arms, and

Rhonda stepped in close, bending to hug her back.

"Thank you, young lady. Thank you so much." The old woman whispered.

Wiping her eyes, Rhonda stood straight, ready to accept her punishment. She looked at Scott, and he was smiling. "I am sorry we've orchestrated a bit of a prank here, but your actions need to be recognized because the consequences for my family have been immeasurable. You are an angel to us."

Prank? They're not mad? I'm not in trouble? She didn't know what to say, could only smile, her mouth quivering, her eyes stinging. Her breath hitched.

The man continued to speak. "I have seen some photos of our boat, and I don't know how much of a gift this is, but we want you to have *Better Life*. We know you will care for her and maybe give your own family what that boat gave us."

Rhonda turned to the crowd in front of her, too overwhelmed to speak. She was afraid of what might burst out of her mouth right now if she said anything. Tears streamed down her face. *The boat is mine? It's in rough shape, but a good scrubbing should restore most of it. Ron will be so jealous; this is no little dingy. It's even bigger than Dad's. Is this really happening?* Her parents and friends clapped and cheered. Even Ron was whooping and smiling.

It's happening. Maybe I'll rename her *Resurrection*, because that dead boat has turned out to be full of life.

Terry Groves

Terry Groves writes from his home in Sooke, BC. He grew up in a military family and served for twenty-six years himself. This nomadic life allowed him to live in Ontario and every province west. It also helped him travel around the world. He retired, went back to school, then enjoyed a second career with the government of British Columbia.

Terry has dabbled with screenwriting and movie making, was a founding member of the VI Film and Entertainment Cooperative. A short movie, Rocket Candy, that he wrote and directed, is on YouTube as are others he worked on.

He blogs about his childhood on www.beingabrat.com and helps with a variety of writing projects. Assisting other writers to hone their craft is also a passion. Visit him on his website www.terrygroves.com. He is a member of Sooke Writer's Collective and Federation of BC Writers.

(photo credit: Mark Laurie)

Plummerias Don't Wilt
by Yana Spencer

Aromas of musky frankincense and cleansing myrrh, burned on every corner, waft through the labyrinths of the ancient souq. White dishdashas of men and black abayas of women move graciously around like chess pieces on a board.

A frail grandfather is setting his tamarind out in a floor display, getting ready for the tourists coming straight from the cruise ship across the road. The sea is calm today – you can only hear a few seagulls fighting over the fish, accidentally dropped from the boats of fishermen.

Behind the shiny front part of the souq, divided by a narrow, tiny street, there is a hidden part of market, only known to locals, full of salons of bright wedding wear, embroidered golden and red for the *Al Baloushi* tribe, fabric shops with all shades of black for elegant abayas; kiosks for men's *kumas*, ornamented in every traditional Omani style; gold shops with big crowds of extended families inside each one, choosing weighty wedding presents for brides; chaotic henna tattoo sticker stalls manned by young female entrepreneurs...

Somewhere, at end of the lane, where kids of all ages queue to buy freshly made *loqaimat* – deep fried pastry, smothered in date syrup, leaving tell-tale sticky brown prints on their white robes, in one of the oldest houses, lives a bit-on-the-heavy-side grandmother.

Her house is a typical construction of Oman's pre-renaissance era (before the majority of the roads, schools and hospitals of the sultanate were built) with a beautifully carved wooden door, small reception *majlis* and a small stove-dominated kitchen, tucked up behind the main house. Here, inside this tiny hut, is where all the magic happens - this kitchen is like an alchemist's laboratory, filled with jars holding secret mixes of Omani marinades for different types of meat and occasions. Her faded navy-blue floral *kandura* and *sirwal* bear turmeric and saffron stains going back many-many years and countless meals, to another life, when her husband was still alive, and the kids were little. How many Ramadans, Eids, birth and wedding dishes were cooked under this mudbrick vaulted roof?! Alongside her black-bottomed metal pots is another witness of her old life - a tall plumeria growing outside her cooking lab. White flowers with yellow honey centres fall chaotically on the bare concrete ground, and the gorgeous lemony scent never fails to take her back to memories of younger years. Mariam, her oldest daughter, would draw henna for celebrations for all the girls from their extended family here under the tree; her boys would hide here from her husband after every committed mischief. As for herself, she had always found the fresh aroma of the white flowers refreshing during the nauseous part of each pregnancy.

'*Jadati*, how many times did dad tell you not to sit under the hot sun?! You have high blood pressure!' – shouts her grandson, waking her from dreams of the past.

'I am grinding cardamom under the tree, Aboodi. It's quite shady here'.

'Still, I shall tell Daddy!'

'Plumerias don't wilt, Aboodi. They belong to the sun. That's why your grandfather planted it here, in the middle of the sunniest spot of our yard. He used to call me plumeria too - because I love the warmth so much'.

'That's why you refuse to move from this house, Jadati! Because of this old tree! I shall tell Daddy that too!'

Grandma sighs and continues pressing her pestle against the mortar.

"Aboodi, listen to me. It's not because of the plumeria", says grandmother, but Aboodi is already running away towards the mountain, where the older boys are playing football.

"Jadati, I am tired listening about your old tree! I want to play FUDBAL (Omani accent)".

You can hear the "fudbal" echoing in the mountains surrounding the souq...

Glossary
Kuma – a rounded Omani cap, traditionally worn by men
Majlis – Arabic for a sitting room
Kandura – a long-sleeved, ankle length garmet
Sirwal – a form of baggy trousers
Jadati – Arabic for Grandmother

Yana Spencer

Yana is a British-Ukrainian journalist and women's rights activist. She runs Tamu, a non-profit organisation which empowers vulnerable women and girls around the world through baking therapy. She splits her time between working with women, training staff at international NGOs about women's rights and gender-based violence, as well as writing. Her literary work, like her charitable work, focuses on women's experiences – frequently through the medium of food. From the deserts of Rajasthan, to the plains of the Maasai Mara, the mountainous coast of Oman and the bustling streets of Hanoi – Yana takes her readers on a journey of discovery of women's lives.

https://matadornetwork.com/read/tamu-bakery-helping-empower-women-around-world/
https://www.youtube.com/watch?v=P_4JbkQ5Y68

Pulling Weeds
by Sébastien Streit

Why was he on the bus? He owned a car. Maybe some inner urge to remember where he came from had overtaken him. He knew he was entering a humbling situation that would set him aback yet once again. He chose not to venture into the vicinity of this place, but he had been called to join them: an opportunity he did not want to let pass. Rarely did he find himself with this type of chance, unlike years past when it was more of a weekly ordeal. Conflicted with his decision, he deemed it was for the best. He almost needed this. A need he hadn't felt in ages.

He pushed the red button and listened for the sound amongst the crowd. He pushed it again to make sure. The sun had been beating down on him through the window, and he had started sweating. The bus pulled to a stop at the side of the road, and a few people exited the vehicle through the back door. Pushing his way from the end of the bus, he barely made it off. The lack of spatial awareness on public transit bothered him. He stepped off the bus, and the city air washed over him. He coughed due to the overwhelming amount of vehicle exhaust. The sounds of the street filled his ears. He could barely hear himself think over the hundreds of cars' engines. The city was too loud for him. He preferred the countryside, where the bird calls and gusts of wind through the trees create a soothing environment. The city was chaotic. He set off down the sidewalk.

He could feel the moisture accumulating under his cotton shirt; his woolen sweater was not helping. He could feel his clothes sticking to him as he walked briskly down the sidewalk. He was to turn right, down the next alley, and walk a while south. Minutes later, he was covered in soot and mud, and he could no longer see the colour of his boots. He was nervous. He hadn't been to this part of the city in at least a year; prior to that, it had been five. Pausing just before the alley, he contemplated heading back. It was difficult for him to walk here. The memories pained him.

He remembered scrounging the ground

for anything that would help him escape, but every time he indulged, he would make escaping that hell closer to impossible. Months he had spent here dying. His spirit was but scraps, lost in the darkest corners of the alley, unrecoverable, or so he thought. An angel had visited him once and offered him a new way of life. He accepted and never looked back. Now, years later, he wondered to himself what was his true purpose of returning to this hole. Had he returned to offer a helping hand to another caught in this deadly cycle?

He turned into the alley. Morbid and gray were the colours of this morgue. People were lying everywhere. The cardboard beds, the ripped tents, and the broken needles scattered on the ground made his skin crawl. There was a man sitting behind a dumpster trying to light a cigarette while the woman next to him was struggling to heat her spoon, both only a few meters away from a busy street in the city. He turned around and watched from the alley as countless people passed by, too busy with their daily lives to look down this path. He spun around and set off. He passed at least fifty people in the first minute of walking. Dissociated from the world around them, struggling to stand, they stared right through him as he trudged along through the alley. He did not walk too fast nor did he walk too slow, avoiding any unwanted attention, but it was to no avail. His hair was well groomed, he was cleanly shaven, and his black leather jacket and crisp blue jeans clashed with everything around him. He had been there. He had walked that path before. He empathized and held no judgment of these people stuck in the alley, yet he couldn't find the courage to reach out to them. He had an *appointment* to get to, and he was running late.

He looked at his wrist. Why did he wear his expensive watch for such an outing? It read 15:31. He had fourteen minutes to get there if he was to be on time. His damp clothes had cooled off as the sun could not peak through the concrete jungle he had entered. His jeans had an icy touch with every stride he took as they had dampened due to his sweat. With his head up, he continued to walk the alleyways, passing yet another group of them. The stench of cigarette smoke hung thickly in the air, mixed with the scent of improperly bathed individuals. He began breathing through his mouth as he was becoming nauseous.

One of the battered tents, only held up by a rope tied to a pipe hanging above the alley, burst open as a man stumbled out, gripping a knife while mumbling incoherent words. He slashed open a few ripped black garbage bags just outside the tent, scouring frantically as if his life depended on it. Pure desperation was a difficult sight to take in. Lifting his gaze, he noticed the colourful graffiti that stretched down the alley. It was illegible for the most part, but one word stuck out as the paint was a deep red: *help*.

Someone screamed. A woman with a white coat came running around the corner, followed by three hobbling men cursing her name. She bumped his shoulder as she flew by, and he caught the scent of her perfume. He loved the scent of roses. It reminded him of springtime in his mother's garden. How often he would find her pulling the invasive weeds, grooming her backyard to hide the imperfections of nature that incessantly returned. How simple life was back when he was under the care of his mother. The undying love he shared for her could not be matched. After her passing, he stormed his way into oblivion, becoming a societal weed stubbornly growing through the concrete. His roots were pure, but nothing beautiful grew from them as he tainted everything with his desire. It was truly a miracle that he was still alive.

They couldn't catch the lady in the white coat; she had clearly taken a wrong turn and didn't know how to act in this part of town. One must stay calm. He contemplated getting involved, but it was none of his business. 15:38, seven more minutes until he was late. What would they think if he was late? Would they still be there? Are they even there, or has he been misled? He was determined to find out.

Picking up his pace now, he knew he only had a few more blocks to go, and the time was now 15:40. His anxiety was growing as he genuinely could not be late. Someone pushing a grocery cart full of recycling bags crossed his path. There was probably around four or five dollars worth of recycling, discarded gold being transported from the depths of a mine. He had to jump to the side to avoid getting hit. A collision would be most unfortunate. This man was wearing a hood and was slouched over the handle of the cart, his shoelaces untied, and the bottom of his shoes scraping against the concrete as he appeared to lack the strength or coordination to lift his feet. The squeaking wheel of the cart was almost rhythmic as the pace of the cart was unaltered as it slowly made its way down the alley. He had stared long enough. The striking presence of guilt overtook him, and he turned back on course.

15:42. He could see the house if one could call it a house. It was in the distance at the crossroad at the end of the alley. Only two more blocks to go. There was clothing hung between the buildings; torn and ragged, much of it was stained, if not by blood, then by filth. He heard quickening footsteps. He looked behind him and saw someone following him. The man seemed distraught and was holding a glass pipe. His other hand was in his coat pocket. What was he to do? He didn't want to start a confrontation in this place. Fear struck him, and his blood boiled, but he was ready to defend himself. To his relief, the man walked straight past him and banged on a wooden door hanging only by one hinge, shouting to be let in. The small sliding door in the center of the entry quickly opened, and the man inside began an interrogation.

It was now 15:44, and he was at the base of the stairs which led up to the rendezvous point. Each step he took was cautious as the boards creaked with the shifting of his weight. There were only about half of the steps left, and he had to climb acrobatically. Opting to avoid the handrail, as it was coated with rust, he danced his way up. If only climbing out of the depths of despair was as easy for the people he passed by as these simple steps. He looked back and gazed down the path he had walked. Many do not see the suffering he had witnessed in the last fourteen minutes of his walk. The pain in his heart was growing, for he had not offered his hand to aid a single soul.

This used to be his getaway, his saving grace from the constant sense of impending doom that loomed over him daily. Stuck in misery, this was a haven for his spirit. In this paradise, he could let go of worry and have fun, at least, until everything turned sideways. It became a place he needed to come to. Every morning, the urge became stronger. Waking in different parts of the city only to stumble his way back to this door was his sole desire. He was sure there weren't many left that used to frequent this door. If they let him in, would he recognize a single face? If their rules hadn't changed, tardiness was not an option, and he would be turned away. He remembered the desperate faces he'd had to reject at the door, the screams of displeasure, and the violence that would ensue.

Why did he come here? The peeling crimson paint on the side of the exterior of the building, the jagged glass in the broken windows, and the stench of urine on the deck before the door were clear signs that this may not be the safest of locations to meet a friend of a friend. But so desperate had he become that he found himself in the most ravaged neighbourhood of the city with three thousand dollars strapped to his back. 15:45, he knocked four times on the door.

Sébastien Streit

Sébastien, a musician and poet, focuses primarily on structured poetry while writing. However, in recent times, he has shown far more interest in longer structures of literature. He is from the Comox Valley on Vancouver Island and has a love of nature and music. As a poet, he mainly writes for cathartic release, but his newer works draw upon themes of nature and love, avenues he hasn't thoroughly explored. Inspired by the beauty of our world and the love shared by many in his life, he continues to write. Exploring these lengthier forms of writing proves a challenge, which he embraces as he tackles short stories and a novel.

Son-of-a Bitch
by Allan Jefferson Reid

***WARNING: some images may be disturbing**.*

The refugee camp sat on agricultural land a few kilometres outside the small town of Chajul, in the southern province of Chiapas, Mexico. It was just five kilometres from the Guatemalan border. The camp housed about a thousand refugees in tightly clustered shacks of corrugated tin and tarps held together with bits of scavenged wood. Narrow, snaking paths, worn to dirt, became muddy when it rained and provided both access and sewage disposal. Each shack was no more than two metres by two metres, was devoid of furnishings, and sheltered as many as ten people, many children. Everyone slept on blankets strewn across bare dirt floors. There were few toilets, no showers, and only very primitive cooking amenities. Water, in insufficient quantity, had to be trucked in. The refugees were mostly unwashed and wore the same filthy clothes day after day. Mexican authorities strictly restricted access to these camps, and foreign media were kept particularly far away.

In the late spring of 1983, I was serving as an Oxfam relief worker at Chajul when Bruce's group arrived. I can tell you that I was quite excited, for I am a huge fan. Bruce is one of Canada's greatest lyric poets. Sometimes satirical, always pointed, his poetry is infused with a liberal consciousness that attacks Western complacency in a world filled with human tragedy. Songs like *Going to the Country* (1970), *It's Going Down Slow* (1972), *All the Diamonds in the World* (1974), *Laughter* (1978), *Tokyo* (1980), *Lover's in a Dangerous Time* (1984) and, perhaps, his most famous, *Wondering Where the Lions Are* (1979) have long been familiar sing-a-long radio tunes even among people who pay no attention to a song's message.

He arrived in camp, his blond hair cropped short, with a large entourage, but hardly the constellation of personalities one expects to fill a rock star's bus. It was three buses, actually, crammed with the modern-day hippie type. Young, mostly. Educated. Middle-class do-gooder recruits not afraid to get dirty. Folks he'd invited to enrich Oxfam's ranks. Chajul was just one of several camps, and these volunteers were soon sifted out among them. Bruce, of course, was a hero among the camp administrators, but he was no prima donna. One might find him slopping out the daily gruel, or in a walkway shovelling shit into wheelbarrows, or helping to clean and disinfect wounds too minor to require a doctor's attention, or, often, just sitting and chatting with the survivors, often with his guitar. All ages, refugee or relief worker, everyone loved Bruce. He had a comforting, compassionate manner that inevitably drew smiles. To some, Bruce's time in Chajul, despite his good work, looked a lot like the stereotype liberal-conscious rock star playing at paying attention—*see how good I am. If only there were cameras about*—but he listened.

To be fair, though I was a volunteer, I was not entirely authentic, myself. I was a freelance journalist collecting stories undercover. I had already collected hundreds of covert interviews, on thousands of pages.

Stories that detailed rapes, torture, murders and wholesale slaughters. In addition, I had cultivated a contact on the Oxfam medical team, a young nurse horrified by what she was seeing, who desperately wanted the world to understand what was happening to the Mayan people of Guatemala. She had access to documented cases of thousands of war-related injuries, though it was easy enough for anyone to see the evidence of what she reported.

Refugees came daily to camp with wounds still gaping, bullets or shrapnel sometimes still lodged within, festering. Young girls came pregnant. Many torn and battered by their rapists. And so many wounds were horribly infected, having travelled, perhaps hundreds of kilometres afoot, without even the most basic medical supplies, just to reach the relative safety of Mexico. All of this, I was quite honoured to share with Bruce.

For Bruce had another, more personal objective at Chajul. To collect impressions of Guatemala's suspected ethnic cleansing of the Mayan people. Impressions, which he hoped, would fuel public anger. Neither Guatemala, nor Mexico, seemed eager to let such stories be heard. Nor was the US, which was deeply embroiled in the conflict for its own purposes, of course. Uncaring of the local population while reassuring the American public with outright lies and plenty of half-truths. Bruce wanted compelling stories. Impetus for a new song. One he hoped would resonate with the North American public. One to expose the atrocities to which their own governments were mostly turning a blind eye.

Notice where I said "relative safety." I had been chafing against that safety for months. A collection of rules dictated how we interacted with refugees. Rule number one was to never be alone with a refugee. Always have a witness. That rule was unnecessary for Bruce, for he was always surrounded by people. Two in particular followed him everywhere. Another rule was that we were not permitted to actually enter Guatemala. This rule, Bruce despised almost from his first day.

Fan that I was, I was nevertheless impressed that Bruce possessed an acute journalists' instinct for tracking down a good story. He almost intuitively sensed that the safety measures were intended as much to insulate the administration and involved governments from criticism, as to actually protect individual volunteers. Those rules allowed some heat to pass, but shielded the world from the full intensity of the horrors of that war, and the atrocities that were occurring daily just a few kilometres to the south. As a journalist, I knew: it is all well and good to collect large quantities of anecdotal accounts and case studies, but there is no better story than one personally experienced. And from Chajul, where one could smell stories rising from the wounds, one could also smell them wafting across that acrid border, and Bruce could smell his song. He was only mildly interested in my notes, preferring to interview sources himself, and the stories we collected whetted our appetites for full immersion, intensified our anger and our determination to take the real story to the world. To implicate not just Guatemala and

Mexico, but the US and even the complacency of Canada, as well.

Bruce had been in Chajul only a week when he approached me outside a volunteer's latrine. Though he encouraged me to think it over, I agreed on the spot, and three days later, with his impressively circumspect videographer John Watson, and photographer Jessica Howard, we slipped secretly out of camp on foot and stealthily crossed the Guatemala border, staying away from the main roads, being careful to avoid the Guatemalan border patrols.

We reached the village of Tierra de Gracia, just nine kilometres southeast of Chajul, just before daybreak. Already people were about, hauling wagon loads of goods to the town's central market where they claimed their habitual spots and busily set up enticing displays of agricultural goods and products. The market was a festival of motion, colour, texture, sound and aroma. Women wore brightly coloured, intricately patterned dresses with full skirts and often thick ribbons of fabric plaited into long braids. Men wore shirts and pants no less colourful or patterned. Tables were piled high and surrounded with boxes of fresh fruits, vegetables, herbs and peppers, barrels of ground chilis and corn and dried beens, freshly baked breads and sweet treats, jugs of fresh milk and local home brews, there were hot tamales and empanadas, and crates of live chickens and snakes. Each table was sheltered from the sun by a colourfully patterned fabric stretched across four poles affixed to the tables below. Arriving customers invariably carried a bag or basket that they filled with this and that while a live band filled the air with spirited music.

We chose Tierra de Gracia because many of the Chajul refugees told us that they had passed through this town, and had received aid to cross the border into Mexico. We suspected, therefore, that Tierra de Gracia might be a target for Guatemalan reprisals, for the official policy was that every refugee was a guerrilla warrior on the evidence that only guerrillas had a need to escape Guatemalan authority. And it was the duty of Guatemalan forces to kill every guerrilla. Of course, anyone who assisted refugees was also deemed a guerrilla, so we expected something would happen at Tierra de Gracia. We did not expect it to happen quite so soon as it did.

The hubbub of Spanish voices haggling, laughing, greeting and arguing diminished slowly at first. The quiet coming on almost imperceptibly. I sensed it first as a vague feeling that something was not quite right. I could see that Bruce noticed it, too. Then, everything stopped. The band, too. And in that sudden silence, ears pricked up, and people listened. A distant thumping. For a brief moment, no one moved as everyone tried to ascertain whether the sound was approaching, or going away. And then, pandemonium.

Only a few heartbeats passed between that silence and the moment the gunship passed over town. Everybody scattered before the staccato rattle of its guns, often tripping over others in their haste to find safety. John and Jessica, with their cameras always ready, slipped into the shadows between two buildings. Bruce and I were among many who practically dove into a nearby storehouse. We crouched into the corners as best we could, staying away from the windows. The terrible chatter of the guns echoed remorselessly as the chopping of its rotor moved audibly from one end of the village to the other and back again. Every scream was a knife in the hearts of our shelter-mates, for inevitably, they were the screams of family and friends. Perhaps they had not managed to find shelter soon enough, or their shelter had proved inadequate. Our shelter was awash in tears, wailing and mumbled prayers, and yet, we all listened intently, trying to place that chopper. If it was behind the storehouse, we clustered against the front wall, If it moved in front, we crossed back again. When it moved away, we exhaled; when it came back, we tensed. Then, the distant screams burst around us as the front wall erupted in a spray of fine dust and projectiles. Those closest to it flooded toward our opposite wall. Several stumbled and fell, some lying motionless. In fact, that building offered poor shelter, for the high-velocity bullets fired from gunships are barely slowed by the concrete blocks of which all village buildings were constructed.

As quickly as it came, the gunship departed, leaving behind an eerie stillness that lasted only a few moments, but seemed to stretch into hours. Nobody moved, either for fear of the gunship returning—hiding to lure them out—or simply because their anguish was too great. But then, in an instant, the floodgates gave way. Some rushed for the doors, anxious to escape into the forest behind the village, hoping to make their way home, perhaps to their farmhouses, praying to find their families safe. Others rushed to the fallen. In our room alone, seven were dead, and more than a dozen had suffered serious wounds from bullets or flying shards of concrete. Bruce and I, both St. John's Ambulance trained and only slightly scratched, did what we could to help the living, which was not much. Mostly, we made tourniquets and bandages from brightly coloured strips we tore from the clothing of the dead, tying them into place. John and Jessica dropped in briefly to capture the carnage and our efforts on film, then excused themselves before disappearing back into the village. I noted an old man desperately trying to console and tend to a terrified boy. Man and boy wore the same festively coloured shirt of oranges, yellows and reds. The boy was holding a bloody hand to one eye, blood dripping down his arm, and onto his shirt. The old man also noted our interaction with John and Jessica.

It was only the briefest exchange of glances that we shared, for soon others arrived to assist the wounded, carrying or supporting them to another building, several doors away, which had been adopted as an impromptu medical clinic, though it was almost completely lacking supplies. Bruce and I, relieved of our duties, walked out into the sunshine, surprised that it was still morning, and a beautiful day. Meeting up with John and Jessica again, we wandered about the village, searching for, but hoping not to find, something useful to do. Corpses lay everywhere. Some where they had fallen. Others pulled from bullet-riddled buildings. These were placed, side-by-side in the sunlight, for families to identify, and to wail over. Terrible to hear. We wondered aloud how many were true guerrillas. One young boy, perhaps eight, lay in the shadows between two buildings, a space only a small boy could have wiggled into. His young body ripped open and his ragged shirt dark with blood. Was he a guerrilla? We found an old woman, slow of foot, crumpled beneath a mud-brick wall spot-stained red above her. Was she a guerrilla? A teenage boy lay sprawled in the grass where he had been mowed down as he ran for shelter in the forest. Perhaps he was a guerrilla, but who knew? Did the gunman in the gunship know? John, Jessica, Bruce and I recorded these finds in our own ways, as we helped carry the bodies into the street, laying them alongside the others. We had just deposited the teen when the old man from our shelter approached.

His name was José, and he was a village elder. He said that he had noticed our early arrival at the market, and wondered about our intentions. He had identified Bruce as our leader, and it was to him that he spoke directly, brusquely demanding to know the nature of our business. Bruce, fluent in Spanish, explained our intentions to document, first hand, the terror that the Guatemalan forces were inflicting upon the rural Mayan people. He explained his own fame as a musician in North America, particularly in Canada, but also in the US. And he explained that he hoped to find a song, and to produce a music video, that would resonate with the North American public. José was skeptical. Who in North America knew or cared about his people? And what right had we, or he, to raise vain hopes of sympathetic ears and helpful voices from beyond. Still, he did not turn us away, or order us to leave Tierra de Gracia. Instead, he gave several hours to Bruce, sitting cross-legged under a tree, while John, Jessica and I captured the conversation. The boy, about fourteen, was one of José's grandchildren, and he stayed close, listening intently but silently as Bruce and José talked. His once festive shirt had been removed to be torn into strips, one of which, the same orange, yellow and red as his grandfather's shirt, was tied around his head, where it held in place another strip that was knotted and pressed against his wounded eye. His name, too, was José.

José senior related that this was the second attack on the village in two months. The first had been by a convoy of jeeps that had swept into town. Young men sitting up behind the driver had shot at anything that moved: dogs, sheep, children. He related that the old woman, whom we had found dead against the wall, whose name had been Gracia, and who had been a great-grandmother to twenty-six of the village children, had been raped by those soldiers on that day, as had many other women and girls, some of whom were now pregnant: one of whom, a granddaughter of his own, Serena, was barely thirteen. The few young men and boys who remained in the village were lucky to have been with their mothers or fathers away from town when the attack occurred or, somehow, to have escaped unnoticed. His stories were identical to ones that we had heard many times at Chajul. I asked him what help was most needed in his village.

"I want the helicopters, and the jeeps, and the guns to go away, and to leave our village at peace," he said, "so that we can be happy again, raising our crops, tending our animals, and enjoying the blessings of this earth."

But his wish was drowned out by the sound of another rotor, or perhaps the same one returning. Once again, folks scattered. Leaving the dead exposed in the road. Bruce, young José and I helped José senior to his feet, and we all rushed to dive into a nearby irrigation ditch, laying ourselves flat against the muddy earth, praying fervently for the gunship to go away. This second attack lasted a further ten terrifying minutes, and left many more dead or injured, among them the old man José, who took a bullet in the back of his head as he ran behind us, even as young José desperately tried to drag him to safety.

The young boy's cries of anguish reached us in our ditch, but we dared not climb out to reach him. We found him in the aftermath, miraculously unscathed, weeping over his grandfather's crumpled body. Bruce knelt beside the boy, his own tears flowing as anger welled inside of me, and I could feel it welling in Bruce, too. We had known the old man only a few hours, but we had already recognized a good man, a gentle man, a man whose only wish was for peace. Bruce placed a hand on the bony shoulder of his thin, shirtless, pubescent grandson. José wiping tears from his good eye with the back of his hand, turned a face of pure hatred toward Bruce. "If I had a rocket launcher," he spat in Spanish, "some son-of-a-bitch would die."

I watched as Bruce lowered his head, clasping the boy more tightly. I had my story, and John and Jessica had their images, many of which would be featured in the disturbing MTV video for Bruce's new song.

Allan Jefferson Reid

Allan Jefferson Reid currently resides in Esquimalt, British Columbia, Canada, where he is best known for his monthly restaurant reviews in Monday Magazine, an imprint of Black Press. Allan, an avid reader, came to writing late in life, discovering, to paraphrase Groucho Marx, that he wouldn't want to read any book he had written. A revelation that led him to pursue a Bachelor of Arts degree, majoring in English, from Athabasca University. Allan is also a lover of the art of music and songwriting and, consequently, a big fan of Bruce Cockburn, and especially his song If I Had a Rocket Launcher. Allan lives and travels with Dennis, his husband of thirty-four years.

The Sea Pool
by S. M. Perkins Carr

Joseph stepped along the concrete wall, his arms stretched away from his body, leaning left, over the old sea pool, and then right, over the Salish sea, daring gravity to take him. Two crabs scuttled sideways in the algae-ridden water held in the rocks. Had they been born there, he wondered, or had they scrambled in from the open ocean?

He turned to the sea, and again imagined jumping from the wall, nearly eight feet down to the waves. How deep was it? Were there rocks beneath the surface?

His phone buzzed in his pocket, interrupting his questions and nearly throwing him off-balance. He ignored it. It wouldn't be Sandra, and there was no one else he wanted to talk to right now. He closed his eyes, willing their last conversation out of his mind, which only brought the words into sharper focus.

"Did you really think we'd stay together if I'm going to university in Toronto in September?"

She'd shaken her head, as if it was simple. As if he should have known. But he hadn't.

As his phone finally relented, Joseph sat down on the wall, his legs dangling above the ocean. The tide rushed in, the sound of waves filling his ears. His gaze moved upward, searching for the moon, but the sky was an empty blue basin. The connection between the moon and the ocean was more nuanced than that, he knew. He knitted his brow, trying to recall the details. The sun was involved, he remembered, as well as currents, even the shape of the coastline. It was a hopeless tangle of relationships too complex to un-weave.

He remembered asking his physics teacher whether humans might have tides, whether the water in our bodies might be subject to the movements of the moon. She'd smiled patronizingly and assured the class that a human was far too small to feel the moon's gravitational pull. He'd sat back in his chair and scowled. She hadn't asked, and she would never know his best stories were always born under a new moon.

The ocean began to envelop the rocks at the end of the beach, the tides an endless hungry monster that approached and withdrew, advanced and retreated. Soon, it would block his path homeward. But he didn't mind. Joseph laid down along the wall, imagining he was trapped here for the night, asleep on the boundary between two worlds. He imagined all the stars he couldn't see in the summer-blue sky, a million worlds circling relentlessly.

Something slipped from his pocket, and he sat up abruptly, his hand rushing to grasp the object. But it was too late. His phone sank into the sea pool, crabs and fish scattering in its wake. "Shit," he muttered to himself as he stared down at it, his legs straddling the wall. He thought about jumping in after it, but the water was murky, green, uninviting, and the phone was likely a lost cause. His mind searched for the expected emotions: annoyance, frustration, panic, but Joseph found only numbness.

He sighed as he imagined telling his parents he'd lost yet another phone. Maybe he could say it had been stolen. Yes, that was it. He smiled slowly, painful resignation tinged with mischief. His phone had been stolen by the neglected sea pool, abducted into its watery world, where, he imagined, it would take on a new life. Instead of its previous offerings of games, social media, text messages of half-truths and over-used emojis, it would now bridge the realms of the isolated pool and the Salish Sea. The water would flow like the messages and memes had, in waves, and the tides would reach ever higher, over the wall and into the sky. The green algae would vanish from the sea pool, the crabs would be set free in the vast ocean, and when the tides subsided, its waters would lie perfectly clear once more.

But, he reminded himself, his smile fading, that was just an outlandish fantasy. The reality was he'd lost an expensive piece of technology that would now be slowly buried in mud. And his parents certainly wouldn't be impressed by his story about the thieving sea pool.

"But what will you *do* with a writing degree?" they'd asked, befuddled, when he'd announced his desire to study creative writing at university. They'd looked from one to the other and then to him, as if trying to figure out which of them had supplied the genetic material for a writer.

He'd shrugged. He'd wanted to study something he enjoyed, but in the face of their constantly furrowed brows and continued questioning, he'd agreed to shift his applications to journalism. Relief for them and a mounting sense of dread for him. Joseph imagined his future, cut off like the sea pool, suffocating slowly.

He leaned over the ocean, looking, as he always did, for clues or remnants of the intake that had once connected the pool to the ocean. Was there an ancient pump somewhere under the waves, that remembered bringing seawater up into the rocky basin? He imagined the broken pipe, clogged with debris, choked like a blocked tear duct.

Joseph looked back towards the sea pool, sweeping his gaze over a sun-bleached log, over to the cracked concrete steps rising up out of the water. He imagined a time before he was born, when families, couples, children, had stepped in and out of the cool seawater, their voices carried on the wind, gleeful screams, secrets shared in lowered voices. But the floundering staircase was now an orphaned relic, disappearing into the leafy trees that blanketed the steep bank behind the pool.

He remembered Sandra, sitting with him on the broken-down steps, her laughter in his ears and his lips on hers.

Were all connections destined to be broken eventually?

He looked at his pale bare feet hanging down from the wall. Did they really belong to him? Maybe they were someone else's, someone who wasn't afraid to jump into the open waters below, someone who was wise enough to understand long-distance relationships never work.

Joseph stood up cautiously and turned to face the ocean. Taking a deep breath in, he looked up at the sky and then down to the waves below him, rising higher against the wall and turning a darker blue as afternoon crept into evening. He moved slowly towards the edge of the wall, an inch at a time, until his toes curled around its edge. He leaned forward, then back, over and over again, angling his body a little more each time, pitting his balance against gravity. Did it matter if he jumped; if he didn't jump? Did it matter if she'd loved him?

One more deep breath. He bent his knees. He closed his eyes. He imagined the force of the moon pulling the tide higher against the wall, pulling his body toward the sky.

He jumped.

S. M. Perkins Carr

Shannon Perkins Carr is an author, poet, and certified music therapist. An experienced songwriter who often dabbled in poetry, she began writing in earnest after dreaming the first line of her debut novel, *Searching for Persephone,* which she self-published in 2022. Since then, she has been following the writing muse, crafting poetry, short stories and a further novel-in-progress, while continuing to work as a music therapist and classical guitarist.

Originally from North Vancouver, Shannon studied composition and guitar at UBC, and went on to complete an MA in music therapy at Anglia Ruskin University, Cambridge. She lived in the UK for ten years, working as a music therapist and charity administrator. In 2019, she returned to Canada's west coast, settling in Victoria.

Her music therapy training and understanding of human psychology inform her explorations of characters and interactions. In her writing, Shannon is interested in portraying characters' internal worlds and the relationships, people and places that define and change them.

The Wishbinder
By P.N.Holland

He leaned over his computer and smiled. *Finally, the story's finished.* He rose from the desk, feeling like a load had been lifted. *A walk would be just the thing.* Out of his room and into the hall, he grabbed his coat and hat and scanned the room.

Looking at the picture of him and his wife on the mantle, he thought of their relationship over the last thirty years, and his shoulders sagged at the memory of the strained feelings between them, the unsaid words. They hardly talked anymore. He couldn't remember the last time they were intimate. *Did she even know that he was lonely?*

He enjoyed the little things like watering the plants, changing a light bulb, washing the dishes or working in the garden, *his* garden. Yet, he felt conflicted. *I am tired of this life. I feel like a piece of furniture in this cookie-cutter house. There must be more to life. I need something else.*

He opened the front door and stepped slowly out. He stood on the threshold, feeling like a departing visitor. A few steps down the path, he glanced back. The grey stone house sat like all the rest of them, cold and uninviting. *I wouldn't miss this dismal life. Would anyone even care if I disappeared?* He sighed, turned, and his feet carried him up the street and along the road. The fresh air hit his face and gave him a new sense of direction. He greeted it with a smile and quickened his pace. *It had been comfortable there. I chose my own routine, made what I wanted to eat, played the games I liked.* Yet, he had no real freedom. He was attached to it all: no purpose, no adventure, no destiny. He was just another human piece in the world's puzzle, not alive just existing. All the relief, the good feelings in his study, had vanished. *Was he already dead?*

An intersection loomed ahead with the woods on one side and the city streets on the other. He looked along the street. Cars zipped by, and the mechanical drone was a painful reminder of what he hated— *the routine, the daily rituals, the boring conversations with robot people in little box houses, all the same. It was so artificial. Some evil god had packaged humanity like a child connecting Lego; one little plastic piece at a time, all linked and perfect.* He hated it. To the left, he saw trees, fields, birds singing overhead and back in the trees — was that a deer? *It was like nature had been pushed aside onto a reserve, so we didn't lose it completely. It wasn't convenient to have it around; just keep it there to look at once in a while.*

He crossed the road and stepped into the field. The sun warmed his face, and the sky appeared bluer here. Along the soft, dirt path, swallows darted about scolding him, telling him to go back to the asphalt world where he belonged. But he persisted, strolling through the meadow where the purples, yellows and reds of daffodils, lilies, crocuses and wild roses waved before him, inviting him to join their colorful dance. The perfume of the foliage welcomed him, and he wished he had been born into another age; one without motors, computers and the ever-present internet, like an invisible God warping their reality. Closer to the trees, he recognized butterflies, robins and jays as they warned the wood of his approach. Insects buzzed in between the stately columns of firs, oak and maple.

He jumped back as a dog raced out, barking at the birds. The owner yelled after it, controlling the dog's natural instincts. *Maybe I should follow my instincts, leave the city and find a place in the natural world.* He passed the woman scolding the dog.

"Good afternoon," he said as he went by. She didn't even look his way. It was as if he wasn't there. He shook his head as he reached the trees. A cool wind welcomed him. He smelled the sweet sap of the firs and marveled at the twisted forms of the red arbutus. The joyful chirping of a robin lilted down from high up in a tree, and he wished he could fly up to it and live there. *It is so quiet and soothing; green and inviting.* As he walked on, he spied a stream. The rustling water whispered to him, *slow down, sit and sleep.* He watched three children build a makeshift dam by piling boulders and small logs in the water. Their laughter and splashing reminded him of his childhood. He perched at the edge and watched the water wind its way deeper into the wood. Reaching down, he cupped the cool, clear water in his hands and tasted its natural flavor. It renewed him, and he stood up. Looking into the depths of the greenery, he saw a flick of white, the tail of a deer? Heading toward it, in hopes of seeing the beautiful animal, brought back a memory.

It was long ago when he was a boy, and he lived by a beautiful, green wood with a creek bubbling through the middle. He used to go there to get away from the craziness of his childhood — the anger and yelling of his father, his mother's tears. His older sister had left the home long before he could, and he felt alone. He remembered the proud, majestic animals standing by the stream, their breath steamy in the morning air. It was beautiful.

One day, his father brought men with big bulldozers, backhoes and dump trucks and in a week, they had destroyed the little wood, filling it in so his father could sell it as another lot. It was all about the money, and he needed lots of it. He didn't care about the animals who lost their homes.

His stomach lurched at the memory. *What had happened to the family of deer?* He still felt guilty and ashamed.

He was closer now; the deer stood with its head cocked, listening for something, smelling something in the wind. It was a three-point, its tail twitched, and its ears were up. It must have picked up his scent. The wood seemed to hush; even the wind died down.

A white tail flashed as the mighty stag leaped behind a tree. In three bounds, it was out of sight. He stood there stunned and disappointed. He wished he'd been more careful. *That was not man's way. He would continue to slash and burn and fill in the woods for more houses to live out his artificial life.* Sitting down on a stump from a fallen tree, the man swished the flies and mosquitoes away with his hat and sighed. Then he smelled the woods again and looked around at the peaceful trees and plants. *This world feels more real than the one I left. I will find freedom here. I wish to survive the way God intended — embracing nature, not destroying it.*

A sharp cry from above and the beat of powerful wings assailed his ears breaking his thoughts. He looked up through the sun-filtered trees. A large shadow swooped down; closer and closer, it spiraled. He stood and took refuge beside a big, red fir. Fear rolled over him like a rash. He breathed slowly, his muscles tense. *Maybe he had been wrong about the tranquil wood.*

"You wish to live in my wood," a harsh voice said. It was more of a statement than a question.

"Y-yes, but who are you?" he stammered, moving slowly out from the tree.

"I am the *Wishbinder* of this wood. I grant wishes to those who desire them. You only have to ask." He could now see a large, bird-like creature with human features, silver wings and claws resting on a large branch above his head.

"What would I have to do in return?" he asked.

"Only be true to your desires, for once you have entered, you can never return. Your wish is final, and you must serve the wood for the remainder of your days."

"Okay, I wish to be a part of the wood." the man said quickly.

"Are you sure?" the creature asked. Its eyes cut sideways, sly and secretive.

The man thought for a moment. *What could be worse than my pitiful reason for existence now? I could be free to live in this beautiful wood with nature at my feet.* He looked up at the Wishbinder. "Yes, I wish to be a part of this wood...forever." *There, I've said it.*

The bird laughed, spread its huge wings and left the branch, spiraling up into the air. "Your wish is granted." Its hollow laughter upset him. *What have I done?* The man looked around; everything looked the same. He felt the same. *How am I different? What is different? What have I become?* He looked for the bird, but it was gone.

Gradually, he noticed that the wood was darkening, and the trees seemed somehow less inviting. The birds shrieked at him, and the wind whipped into his face. He walked quickly back towards the sounds of the city. Doubt seeped into his soul. Maybe it hadn't changed anything. Could he go home; back to his garden, his library and his cozy kitchen? Still, he felt disappointed. *If the spell didn't work, I might as well go home.* He followed the path to the stream. The children had left, but they had built quite an imposing structure to stop the water, which was pooling and rising, ready to flood the bank. He stood and looked at it for a time, caught between intervening and leaving it alone. *If I leave it, it might flood the field and change the course of the stream. This could ruin the wood.* He went to work pulling away the boulders and logs. The water found its natural path and continued on its way as it had been before the children obstructed it.

He smiled and stepped out into the field. The children were kicking a ball, two dogs were chasing them, and a lady was sitting on a blanket. He smiled and walked toward the children. They didn't look at him.

He reached the lady on the blanket. She didn't see him.

"Hello," he said. She did not answer him. "Hello!" he said louder. She did not respond or even look at him. *She can't see me. Am I invisible?*

"Tom, David, Sarah, come and eat!" the mother called to her children. The boys and the dogs immediately stopped playing and ran to the blanket, but the girl was chasing the ball as it headed toward the busy street. He saw a group of cyclists talking and racing along the roadway, paying no attention to the little girl as she ran into the street. He ran through the field in fear, yelling for the girl to stop, but she didn't hear him, and as he reached the roadway, he felt something pull him back toward the wood. He could only watch in desperation as one of the cyclists ran into her. The cyclists stopped, one of them picked her up, and they called to her mother. The family all rushed to the roadside. Sarah was crying but seemed okay. She only had scratches and minor cuts. Her mother carried her to the blanket. The cyclists made sure she was okay before they continued on their way.

What is going on? Why couldn't I help her? The man thought as he watched the family tend to Sarah.

"I told you. You cannot return. You belong to the wood now and must serve it. You cannot interfere with the living, only help them to feel comfortable by caring for the wood."

He looked back and saw the Wishbinder sitting on a tree branch at the edge of the field. The children and the lady didn't seem to notice it.

"But isn't saving someone from harm helping them?" He was feeling more human than he ever had.

"It is not your choice anymore. You relinquished that right with your oath to the wood."

"But she is just a child," the man wailed.

"Enough of this. You have chosen your path," the Wishbinder unfolded and flapped his wings.

"I will serve but not as a prisoner!" he yelled in desperation.

"You have made your choice. Your wish is binding. Come, there are chores to do."

The man cried out and tried to reach the road, but he was pushed back to the trees as if by a strong wind. He wailed louder as he disappeared into the trees.

"I would rather be at home living my boring life than live as a slave!"

The Wishbinder laughed. "You must accept your fate. At least you will have the trees to keep you company."

"But what of my life, my house, my books? I can't just leave it all there."

"You left it as soon as you went out of your front door, don't you remember?"

"Yes, but I was wrong. I want to go back."

"You cannot go back." The Wishbinder flew away toward the field where the children were playing.

Back on the blanket, the woman set out sandwiches, drinks and apples for lunch.

"Mother, did you hear someone?" Sarah asked as she wiped away her tears.

"No, dear, it was just the wind in the trees," answered her mother, caressing her

"But it sounded like someone crying. Can we go for a walk in the woods, Mother? Maybe someone needs help."

"Maybe tomorrow, dear; it's getting late. Eat some supper." The little girl sighed and reached for a sandwich. She looked over to the trees.

"Mom, I'm sure someone needs help," the girl yelled, rose and ran towards the trees.

"Sarah, come back here," her mother called as she rose and followed her.

"I belong in the world of people like this family," the man argued as he watched the lady run after her daughter. The girl had reached the edge of the woods, just a few meters from where he stood. "You should go back to your mom, where you'll be safe," he said.

With his words, the girl stopped and looked around, scratching her head in confusion.

"You can hear me, but you can't see me?" he questioned.

"Yes, who are you?"

"The Spirit of the Woods," he said, trying not to frighten her. "I mean you no harm. Just remember to always treat the natural world with respect and help preserve it for all."

"Oh, I will. I love the trees, birds and flowers here. Sometimes, I even talk to the animals, and it's as if they understand because they're not afraid to let me see and pet them."

"Well, that's a gift. Love them, and they will return your kindness."

"Sarah, what are you doing? Who are you talking to?" her mother asked as she caught up to her daughter.

"The Spirit of the Woods, Mom."

Her mother reached down and wrapped her arms around her daughter. "You have such a vivid imagination, honey. That's nice. But let's get going; the sun is setting, and it will be dark soon. She turned her little girl away from me and led her back to her brothers.

"Bye, Mister Spirit of the Woods," the youngster said, turning her head partially in my direction.

"Bye, dear," I said, watching as they left the trees for the open meadow where her brothers yelled, scolding her for running off.

The Wishbinder smiled. Looking at the man, he said, "Come to the stream, and I will show you why you cannot return." The man hung his head and followed the birdlike creature. He watched as the Wishbinder reached over and touched his claw to the water. The surface flickered with light, and an image appeared. His wife appeared, standing over a desk, *his* desk. A body slumped across it, lifeless. He recognized the clothes, the ring on his finger, *his* wedding ring. *Oh my God.*

The Wishbinder smiled as the image faded.

P. Neil Holland

 Raised in Victoria, BC, Canada, P. Neil. Holland writes in memory of his wife, Kris. He has two children, five grandchildren and two dogs. Neil has taught for over 30 years in Public Schools in British Columbia and holds an M.Ed from the University of Victoria with a major in English. His writing is fast-paced, and his stories are page-turners.

The Vancouver Island Mysteries Series: The Saxe Point Park Mystery, The Lost Boys of Lampson, and *The E&N Escape* are all magical mysteries with settings close to home. He has written a Teacher's Study Guide for *The Saxe Point Park Mystery*, which is being used to teach the novel. He is proud of the fact that his book is helping kids improve their reading and writing skills. Neil also likes to visit schools where he shares his insights on reading and writing with students and teachers. *Vahldohr* – Book One in the *Melilissadorha Series* is his most recent YA book featuring a teenage girl learning about her inherited magical talents.. He is currently working on Book Two in that series, a collection of short stories and a detective series. https://pnholland.com/

Acknowledgements

We are grateful for the interest and participation of many authors not included in this collection. We received so many terrific submissions, and the job of the editorial committee judges was quite tricky. Thank you for your submissions. Please continue to write and explore your talent and skills.
We look forward to seeing more from you all.

Thank you to Ron Kearse, Katie Horricks-King and Kelly Duff for the hours spent reviewing submissions, voting on preferences and giving insightful feedback. Many of the authors commented with appreciation for feedback on their work. The selection process was approached with enthusiasm and diligence.

We also sincerely appreciate the faith and trust invested by our many authors over the past twenty years. We hope to continue to earn a growing role as a mentor and advocate for the Global and Canadian writing communities.

20 Years of Amazing Authors and Great Books

The following are the books Filidh Publishing Corp has published and the authors we have been fortunate to work with since 2003.

Anthologies (multiple authors)

Anthology for a Green Planet (2014) (Astra Crompton, Gordon Henderson, Jessie Blair, Josh MacLeod, Monique Jacob, Vince Galati, Werner Roberts, Zoe Duff)   Royalties to Pedal to Petal.

Blood Moon Rising Anthology (2017) (AB King, Astra Crompton, Brianna Kempe, Janilee Porter-Hirsche, Jessie Blair, Kenton Moore, Monique Jacob, Ron Kearse, Scott R.M. Duff, Thomas Keesman, Zoe Duff) Royalties to AIDS Vancouver Island.

Sharing Our Journeys: Queer Elders Tell Their Stories (2018) (Brian Baxter, Claude Hewitt, Cyndia Cole, Fernando Esté, Greta Hurst, Harris Taylor, Ken Sudhues, Marsha Ablowitz, Michael Yoder, Neil, Fernybough, Pat Hogan, Ron Kearse, Tom Dekker, Val Innes) Royalties to Alexandra House.

Sharing Our Journeys 2: Queer BIPOC Elders Tell Their Stories (2022) (Agustin Restrepo, CJ Jackman-Zigante. Cornell Thomas, Gloria Jackson-Nefertiti, Jayantha Withanage, Neil Fernybough, Oscar Hall Rebecca Mabanglo-Mayor, Ron Kearse and Shinji Kasama) Royalties to Alexandra House.

The Platinum Collection (2023) (Mademoiselle Noir, Sara Ashton, Melissa Moose, Surijan Rupsha Mitra, Daphne Matiza, Monique Jacob, Terry Groves, Yana

Spencer, Sébastien Streit, Allan Jefferson Reid, S. M. Perkins Carr, P. Neil Holland) Royalties to Stand Up To Cancer Canada

The UnValentine Anthology (2015) (AB King, Brianna Kempe, Jessie Blair, Katie Horricks-King, Kelly Duff, Kristoffer Law, Monique Jacob, Pam Desjardine, Peninah Rost, Ron Kearse, S.M.King, Thomas Keesman, Vince Galati, Zoe Duff) Royalties to PEERS.

Short Story Collections (single author)

The Tantra of Chimera (2003) (Zoe Duff)

Erotic Tales (2021) (Kama Tarumi)

Erotic Short Stories (2021) (Kama Tarumi)

Fables, Fictions, and Fantasies: A Compendium (2018) (Chloe Cocking)

Guy Stories (2021) (Richard Beamish)

Inspirational Short Stories (2023) (RP Mickelson)

The Awakening of Ame (2014) (Venetia Black)

The Power of a Flowering Cactus (2021) (Kama Tarumi)

Three's the Charm (2021) (Chloe Cocking)

Adult Fiction

A Matter of Perspective (2009) (2022) (Zoe Duff)

Alone (2016) (K.B. Horricks-King)

Beyond Life (2018) (Victoria Helmink)

Blood Rain (2017) (Chloe Cocking)
Dreaming Gods of Gaia (2021) (Cherokee Freechild)

Dreams of El Dorado (2023) (Gilberto Talero)

Just Outside of Hope (2016)(Ron Kearse)

Lalita's Power, Book 1 of the Mystical Healing Trilogy (2023) (RP Mickelson)

Road Without End (2015) (Ron Kearse)

Star Bright, (2016) (Sheila Tracy)

Stone House (2021) (RP Mickelson)

The Awakening of Meeachan Park (2023) (Elle Hawkweed)

The Jagged Tree (2015) (Kristoffer Law)

Tye Dye Voodoo (2012) (Monique Jacob)

Violent Skies (2017) (T.J. Lockwood)

Voodoo Mystery Tour (2013) (Monique Jacob)

Non-Fiction

Do No Further Harm: Becoming a White Ally in Child Welfare Work with Aboriginal Children, Families and Communities (2014) (Grace H. Atkinson)

Ex Animo (2020) (Ron Kearse)

Exploration of Decision Making Among Child Welfare Social Workers (2014) (Dr. A.M.Clayton)

Lost History (2016) (Ron Kearse)

Love Alternatively Expressed: The Scoop on Practicing Polyamory in Canada, (2015) (Zoe Duff)

Musings of a Housework Avoidance Expert (2023) (Charmaine Welch)

T.A.D.A. – Teenagers Are Darn Amazing! A Teacher's Reflections (2023) (Rick Griffin)

Poetry

A Dance With Fire (2023) (Sébastien Streit)

A Place for the Broken (2022) (Sébastien Streit)

Hector (2019) (Chloe Cocking)

Love and Cheese (2017) (Shannon McEwen)

The Cracks in My Soul (2016) (Shannon McEwen)

UnTethered (2021) (Zoe Duff)

Words That Went Unspoken: Vision of Two Hearts, (2011) (Zoe Duff, JPS Hawksworth)

world without end: poems (2023) (Chloe Cocking)

YA (12 – 20 yr old readers) Fiction

Bright Light (2015) Monique Jacob

Invisible Girl, (2015) (Cherise Craney)

The Vancouver Island Mysteries Series:
      The Saxe Point Park Mystery - Volume 1 (2023)   (P.N. Holland)
      The Lost Boys of Lampson – Volume 2 (2023) (P.N. Holland)
      The E&N Escape – Volume 3 - (2023) (P.N. Holland)

Vahldohr – Book One - Mellissadorha Series (2023) (P.N. Holland)

Children's Books

Mrs. McGillicudy and the Boy Called Fish (2005) (Zoe Duff, Ken McLaren)

Pirates of the Black Rose Activity Book (2023) (Captain Theodora Quillplank)

That's What Teddy Bears Do (2023) (Ron Kearse)

The Adventures of the Infamous Mrs. McGillicudy (2004) (Zoe Duff, Ken McLaren)

The Class Menagerie Series:
    Emerson's Flight (2017) (Zoe Duff)
    Kaida of Fyrefly Hearth (2018) (Zoe Duff)
    Lambie-pie (2006) (Zoe Duff)
    Lambie-pie and Billy Badger (2007) (Zoe Duff)
    Scotty Mouse and the House That Roared
-    (2008)   (Zoe Duff)
    Serenity of the Briar Patch (2023) (Zoe Duff)
    The First Week (2022) (2023) (Zoe Duff)

The Forest Friends to the Rescue (2023) (Zoe Duff)
Nana Ruby and the Forest Friends (2023) (Zoe Duff)

Follow us on Facebook, Instagram, Tik Tok and X/Twitter for new releases and event notices. View details on our books and purchase options at filidhbooks.com or sign up for our newsletter.

Changing Lives with Compassion

StandUpToCancer.ca

Royalty proceeds from the sales of this book will go to **Stand Up To Cancer Canada**.

GIVE FOR LOVE, GIVE FOR LIFE
100% of your donation received by Stand Up To Cancer Canada will support collaborative cancer research, education, and awareness programs within Canada.

WHAT IS STAND UP TO CANCER CANADA?
For too long, Cancer has been the leading cause of death in Canada. It's time to stop Cancer in its tracks. Stand Up To Cancer Canada (SU2C Canada), a program of SU2C Canada aims to build broad support for a groundbreaking "translational" research model that can produce meaningful advances in cancer treatment. With the goal of accelerating the pace at which new therapies get to patients, SU2C Canada will enable leading scientists in different disciplines from multiple institutions to work together.

DREAM TEAMS
A distinctive feature of SU2C-funded research is the "Dream Team" concept, in which researchers from different universities or other institutions come together to share resources and data and work collaboratively to develop new and innovative therapies for Cancer. The funds are derived from a nationwide telecast in 2014 that appealed to the Canadian public to pledge support for cancer

research, awareness, and education and from the support of generous collaborating groups.

A call for ideas for research proposals was issued by SU2C Canada after the telecast. The proposals were reviewed by the SU2C Canada Scientific Advisory Committee, composed of leading researchers and co-chaired by Alan Bernstein, OC, PhD, FRSC, President and CEO of the Canadian Institute for Advanced Research (CIFAR), and Nobel Laureate Phillip A. Sharp, PhD, Institute Professor at the Massachusetts Institute of Technology and David H. Koch Institute for Integrative Cancer Research at MIT.

As Dr. Sharp put it, "Cancer is an extremely difficult and complex problem. The Dream Team approach, in which outstanding researchers work together in a collaborative manner, is our best opportunity to move promising treatments from 'bench to bedside' as quickly as possible and benefit the patients who need them so desperately."

https://standuptocancer.ca/the-science/dream-teams/

www.ingramcontent.com/pod-product-compliance
Lightning Source LLC
Chambersburg PA
CBHW050410030726
47503CB00006B/2111